For my mother, Nuzhat Khanum Chughtai, the oldest of Mirza Azeem Baig Chughtai's children.

Through her recounting of memories, she kept him alive for the family as long as she lived, even though he died when she was in her teens.

VAMPIRE

A Novel

Mirza Azeem Baig Chughtai

Translated from the Urdu by

Zoovia Hamiduddin

SPEAKING
TIGER

SPEAKING TIGER BOOKS LLP
125A, Ground Floor, Shahpur Jat, near Asiad Village,
New Delhi 110049

First published by Speaking Tiger Books in 2024

ISBN: 978-93-5447-846-8
eISBN: 978-93-5447-998-4

10 9 8 7 6 5 4 3 2 1

Typeset in EB Garamond by SÜRYA, New Delhi
Printed at Impressions Printing & Packaging Ltd., Noida

Mirza Azeem Baig Chughtai (also written as Chagtai; 12 August 1898–20 August 1941) was a renowned Urdu fiction writer, novelist, humorist and short story writer from pre-partition India. He was one of the earliest proponents of feminism in the Indian subcontinent. He was a champion of women's rights, an activist in the cause of women's rights and freedom, a lawyer who fought pro bono for the rights of women. He eventually also became a chief justice of the high court of the Princely State of Jawara, India. He was a mentor to his younger sister Ismat Chughtai, who in her own right was a renowned Urdu writer of her time who wrote extensively on themes including female sexuality and femininity, middle-class gentility, and class conflict, often from a Marxist perspective. Mirza Azeem Chughtai wrote extensively despite his early death at the age of forty-one. Some of his most well-known works are *Vampire*, *Chamki*, *Shehzori*, and *Quran and Purdah*, to name a few.

Dr Zoovia Hamiduddin is Mirza Azeem Baig Chughtai's granddaughter and Ismat Chughtai's grandniece. She grew up in Peshawar, Pakistan, graduated from Khyber Medical College and did her post-graduate training in medicine from Northwestern University, Chicago. She practices medicine in New Rochelle, New York.

She is the author of a book of short stories titled *Her Mother's Daughter*, and some of her articles and reviews like 'The First Feminist Urdu Writer,' 'Misunderstanding Lihaaf,' 'Chughtai's Timeless, Timely Vampire,' and 'Ismat's Political Allegory' have appeared in the Pakistani newspaper, *Dawn*.

Her translation of Mirza Azeem Baig Chughtai's novel *Vampire* is her first translation project and will be followed by another Chughtai novel, *Chamki*, also to be published by Speaking Tiger.

Contents

Translator's Note

> 'A nation in which the status of women is falsely elevated, but in reality is degraded, will be wiped away from the face of the earth like an unwritten word.'
>
> —*Tafweez: An Extraordinary Dream,*
> Mirza Azeem Baig Chughtai

Mirza Azeem Baig Chughtai was quite possibly the first feminist Urdu writer, calling for women's rights before the words 'activist' or 'feminist' were even formulated. Iconoclastic, anti-cleric, and anti-establishment, he was a literary soldier raising his pen against injustices and atrocities, just as his ancestors had raised their swords against oppression. Maligned, misunderstood, and finally pigeonholed as a humorist—which he indeed was, his short stories 'Yakka' and 'Al Shizri' have been immortalized by the renditions of none other than the legendary raconteur Zia Mohyeddin—he suffered immensely for voicing his support towards ending the sufferings of women.

Every book reveals something about its writer and Chughtai's writings are no exception. Whether light-hearted comedies, satirical plays, religious and social interpretations of the Quran and Hadith [the collective record of the sayings, customs, and practices of the Prophet Muhammad (PBUH) and his companions], poignant short stories, or tragic novels, they all exhibit a continuous theme: an acknowledgement of the dignity of women, a respect for their unique role in society, an empathetic and heartfelt understanding of their downtrodden status, and an unwavering commitment to their rights. Chughtai considered women integral and pivotal to the existence, survival, and progress of any society.

Convinced that the miserable social conditions of the Indian Muslims were directly related to the status they assigned to Muslim women, his first writings dealt head-on with the standing of Muslim women in India and he tried to persuade his readers towards improving it with straightforward interpretations of Islamic law as per the Quran and Hadith. He was naive enough to assume that he could make a difference by enlightening the people, for he believed the Quran was a book of law. In contrast, most Muslims revered it like a talisman: they kissed it, wrapped it in velvet and silk, and put it away on top of a shelf.

Chughtai's first writings as an adult were *Quran Aur Purdah* (Quran and the Veil), *Hadith Aur Purdah* (Hadith and the Veil), and *Raqs-o-Sarood* (Dance of Ecstasy). Their publications were invariably greeted with a hailstorm of angry demonstrations. Newspapers and magazines labelled Chughtai a heretic. The morally righteous were mortally offended, and showered him with death threats. Even though he was not alone in his fight for female emancipation—among his supporters were such illustrious personalities as Hazrat Khwaja Hasan Nizami, the Nawab and Begum of Bhopal, magazines such as *Nairang-i-Khayal*, *Saqi*, and *Ismat*, Shahid Ahmed Dehlavi, M. Aslam, Mullah Wahidi, and the honorable Justice Sir Shah Muhammad Sulaiman (who wrote the introduction to *Quran Aur Purdah*)—Chughtai's forthright approach was ill-received by the conservative public. Alongside the clergy that rose as one against him, many newspapers and writers took his literary daring as a golden opportunity to elevate themselves by pulling him down and tearing him apart. There were street demonstrations, political and religious pressure, attempts on his life, a fatwa declaring his marriage illegal, and finally, a public bonfire of his books.

Chughtai's greatest talent was to be able to enter the dark recesses in the minds of his female characters and voice the thoughts from within so perfectly that readers were convinced the story had been narrated to him by a woman.

Nowhere is this more evident than in his dark, horrifying, and tragic novella, *Vampire*. Long before the #MeToo movement, long before any recognition and acceptance of Rape Trauma Syndrome, long before terms such as 'secondary rape' and 'Stockholm syndrome' were coined, he dared to write about the unpalatable, the unmentionable, the unrecognized subject of rape in a Muslim society and that, too, from the female victim's perspective.

For Chughtai to write about so scandalous a subject at the height of his popularity was literary suicide, but he remained steadfast. He wrote with delicacy and restraint about a young Muslim girl who is brutally violated at the hands of the supposedly virtuous. Through his pen, she tells us her story from behind a veil of tears, of the fight she puts up with all her frail might for her personal dignity. In simple and chaste language, she tells us of the humiliation and shame she suffers, the loneliness of not being able to find solace or help, and of the great lengths she goes to in order to protect her family's 'honour'. The details are so intimate that the reader feels uncomfortable, as if invading the nameless girl's privacy. The candid directness of her 'I' leaves us horrified and repelled, awash with guilt and shame.

In an interview with his friend, editor, and publisher, Shahid Ahmed Dehlavi—grandson of Deputy Nazir Ahmad, who had himself been ruthlessly persecuted by the pious gentry of pre-Partition India—Chughtai declared that he very often did not give his main characters or protagonists any names. He left that to the readers' imaginations, allowing them to give the characters whatever names they chose, because 'it makes the characters more human and personal and the readers can identify with them better.'

I had avoided reading *Vampire* for as long as I can remember. By the time I gathered the courage to read it as an adult, the #MeToo movement had begun gathering momentum in the world. The news on television featured women speaking up about sexual assault, and the pain, anger, and helpless frustration they had borne for so long was mirrored in the pages of the tattered book in my hands. Published by Jahangir Book Depot, Khari Boli, Delhi, Chughtai's preface is dated November 24, 1932. Eighty-six years later, life was still imitating art and *Vampire*, written in colonial Delhi, was resonating in the pages of *The New York Times*, while Facebook, Twitter, and every modern social media platform available were flooded with harrowing tales from women who had survived sexual assault.

The intuitive sensitivity, exquisite sympathy, and depth of understanding might make a reader forget that this is the work of a nineteenth century Muslim man. Imagine that. Chughtai was writing about Rape Trauma Syndrome and the stages of anguish a survivor goes through in the 1930s. The West first described and recognized Rape Trauma Syndrome in 1974.

But before we venture into the story, it is important to examine the title. Chughtai hailed from a literary family. His maternal grandfather, Munshi Umrao Ali (Usmani), was a famous writer of his time. He wrote the novel *Razm Bazm*, a satirical play called *The Ilbert Bill*, and translated William Shakespeare's *Hamlet* into *Jahangir*. Chughtai's father, Mirza Qaseem Baig Chughtai, was among 'Aligarh's First Generation'—the first seven students to graduate from the newly minted Aligarh Muslim University. In 1912, Mirza Qaseem was awarded the title of Khan Bahadur (conferred by the Government of British India on Muslim subjects in recognition of services rendered) at the Delhi Durbar.

Like many belonging to the educated classes of pre-Partition India, Chughtai was familiar with the work of Western writers. Historically, Gothic horror novels were being written in England in the eighteenth and nineteenth centuries and were extremely popular. Irish author Bram Stoker's *Dracula* was published in 1897, and up until the 1900s authors such as H. Rider Haggard, Rudyard Kipling, Robert Louis Stevenson, Arthur Conan Doyle, and H.G. Wells were publishing stories in which fantastic creatures threatened the British empire. Even Jane Austen, the queen of drawing-room dramedies, dabbled in the genre, albeit with a twist—her *Northanger Abbey* is a satire of Gothic horror. In Stoker's *Dracula*, the male vampire feeds on the blood of young women. Once bitten, the victim never really recovers. She is forever changed, hovering in a limbo, not alive, yet not entirely dead. Her mind and body become prisoner to this demonic entity and as he continues to prey upon her, she is rendered a hollow shell. Death cannot free her; death is not even an option. She can regain her stolen self only when Dracula himself dies, which is impossible since Dracula is, for all intents and purposes, immortal. The evil he inflicts upon his hapless victims is everlasting.

In an echo of this eternal anguish, Chughtai's *Vampire* symbolizes women who enter the realm of the undead as a consequence of sexual assault. Terrorized and traumatized, their very souls in a state of perpetual torment, they, too, are changed forever, rendered neither living nor dead. But unlike *Dracula* and other novels in the genre that displayed a strong anti-foreign sentiment, Chughtai's 'vampire' is not an outsider, but one of our own. Chughtai is pointing out that this soul-sucking fiend has been given birth, and is being nurtured, by conservative Muslim society itself. His story is an allegory for the conditions prevalent in his time when the Muslims of India feared their culture would be corrupted by external influence. Chughtai's allegation, that Islam was not in danger from outside forces, but being destroyed from within by the Muslims themselves, was therefore decidedly unnerving. The sixteen-year-old victim is symbolic of the decaying culture of Indian Muslims; she is lost and helpless, mercilessly ravaged by the very people she mistakenly believes will protect her. Chughtai's 'vampire' is not just a sexual predator, he is representative of the whole of society that blames, shames, and judges the victim.

Today, we call this 'secondary rape'. This term, coined by the West in 1991, was brought to light by Chughtai in 1932. Chughtai further draws parallels between the rape of the young woman with the tragedy of Karbala, which occurred in the first month of the year 61 Hijri [the Islamic calendar as beginning from the year the Prophet (PBUH) migrated from Makkah to Madina]. It might be coincidence that the age of one is the transposed numbers of the age of the other. Then again, it might not.

The virtuous, innocent woman—a child, really—represents the then very young religion of Islam itself, and Chughtai compares the loss of her sense of self to that infamous day in Islamic history when the forces of evil—that were ostensibly its guardians—dealt a harrowing blow to the very character of a blossoming Islam, for which the Islamic world weeps tears of blood even today.

A classic work of literature must have universal appeal, and be able to affect readers to the very core no matter how many years have passed since it was written. The make-up of human nature does not change, neither does humanity—or lack of it. Despite its somewhat (understandably) dated language, *Vampire* is as relevant today as it was nearly nine decades ago, for the curse of sexual violence against women does not seem likely to disappear anytime soon.

Christine Blasey Ford, a doctor of psychology and a

professor at Stanford University, is just one woman among many who can identify with the suffering and silence of the victim of Chughtai's *Vampire*. Although their circumstances differ vastly—one is a cloistered Indian Muslim teenager in the 1930s, the other a mature, highly accomplished, professional, twenty-first century Western woman—all of us who followed Ford's much-publicized testimony against her assailant, Brett Kavanaugh, saw what happens when a woman dares to speak up about sexual assault. Ford was mocked, ridiculed, and verbally stoned by the President of the United States as thousands of Americans chanted 'Lock her up!' Meanwhile, Kavanaugh has gone on to become an associate justice of the Supreme Court of the US.

After reading Chughtai's preface and his interviews multiple times, I have finally realized what he is really saying to society. I have also realized the distasteful compromises that have to be made by survivors of sexual assault. The end of Chughtai's *Vampire* again echoes Dracula; Lucy Westenra cannot escape her blighted fate to live as the bride of the bloodthirsty monster, and Chughtai's heroine—abandoned by family, friends, and society, unable to kill herself or fight the inevitable—makes a most heinous choice that makes the reader recoil. Such choices are made every day even now.

Chughtai's literary career was short, lasting barely fourteen years. A prolific writer and a true Daastaangoh, he wrote in both Urdu and Hindi. Among his many novels are *Shareer Biwi* (The Mischievous Wife), *Maharani Ka*

Khwaab (The Queen's Dream), *Khanum* (Lady), and *Shehzori* (A Woman of Strength), which was serialized into a television play and broadcast by Pakistan Television (PTV) in the 1970s. Chughtai was also a regular contributor to the *Vishal Bharat*, a popular newspaper of its time.

In his brief life—he died at the age of forty-three—he became both extremely popular and controversial. As a lawyer and chief justice of the princely state of Jawara, he fought landmark cases against the prevailing so-called Mohammedan laws in British India to obtain female-initiated divorce for Muslim women. In her seminal essay 'Dozakhi' (Hell-Bound), his sister Ismat Chughtai wrote, 'For me, he is more alive now after his death than he was when he was alive. For what is death anyway? When I look around and see his books, I say to myself: he will never die. He will be born again and again for each new generation of readers, and even for those born after his death. His message "fight the injustice, fight the hate" will never die. His defiant spirit will live on forever.'

Now, more than seventy years after his death, the annual Mirza Azeem Baig Chughtai Memorial symposium takes place at the Maulana Azad University in Jodhpur, India, under the auspices of the university's vice chancellor, Dr Akhtar al Wasi. Chughtai lives on, once more to be rediscovered, resurrected, and read again and again.

This foreword includes some passages taken from articles written by Dr Zoovia Hamiduddin in *Dawn* newspaper

Author's Preface

Deceit alias Vampire: An Apology

In the daily grind of the mundane and the monotonous splitting of hairs in my law practice, I decided to assault the already burdened persona of 'Urdu language'. Once thus committed I rolled up my sleeves and went to work. Dictionaries were torn up, grammatical norms were discarded, proverbs and idioms were shattered. Words were flung about, sentences dismembered, tragedy was decapitated, humour and satire were wrestled to the ground, and then, after much chest-thumping and self-congratulation, I declared, 'See, this is how real, talented writers write a sehra.'

I say to the readers, tear up your sex manuals and burn those how-to books on satisfactory home life and sex science, with their 'Oh so correct' tone and vocabulary, all those books that are brimming with suggestive titles, sexual innuendos, and are in reality pornographic in nature because, I am right in saying that their author has not succeeded. He could not harm Urdu in any way. These books and magazines have not provided any new or useful addition to Urdu and instead Urdu now has been amply enriched with a treasure trove of pornography.

Urdu readers really don't need these books and magazines that have fancy, colourful covers showing fully clothed women with saucy expressions on their faces in suggestive poses, with even more suggestive and downright vulgar pornographic titles and which are presented along with extremely filthy and foul-smelling titles in literary magazines. This is done just to prove that these magazines sell and all those who say the following are liars:

> 'Real connoisseurs of literature know the difference between nudity and vulgarity, between art and obscenity. A picture of a beautiful naked woman is not as titillating as a picture of a fully clothed woman who has been objectified and sexualized, with suggestive pornographic writings, in the most vulgar way. After all, law, religion, medicine and art are filled with nudity, but no one sees it as pornographic. The description of an incident, whether written or verbal or an image, unless deliberately sexualized and poisoned, is in itself not pornography.'

I ask my readers once again, please pay attention to my 'Apology'. After all, what crime have I committed? And is it not the birthright of every Urdu writer to leave barely a hair's space of a distance between literature and pornography? Schoolchildren as young as ten to fifteen years of age, under the guise of guidance, are being exposed to books, magazines, and short stories with completely imaginary, unrealistic, incorrect, improbable, unnatural, trashy, titillating, suggestive, vulgar and romantic dialogue that makes one's head spin. And all this is being passed on as literature and art, as it is written in a technically correct language, without any plausible subject matter. So dear readers, as a writer I too must have such literary licence.

'Vampire' is an English word and I admit I have committed a theft. In my defence let me say that you might have noticed that recently Urdu writers have taken to foraging, fishing for and hunting Arabic, Persian and even Turkish vocabulary? As we are Muslims, we feel compelled to invade the Arabic language with great aplomb. I on the other hand, decided to steal from English. Let me assure you that the Urdu language needs the word 'vampire'. If you have any doubts please look it up in the dictionary. Remember this word is made in England and you won't find it in Iran, Toran, Arabia or Khorasan.

—Mirza Azeem Baig Chughtai,
Jodhpur
24 November 1932

PART ONE

1

Sleep of Death

Oh! King of kings, lord and master of this world and beyond, owner of the day of judgement, I beseech thee to grant me recognition. I beg of thee to listen to my tale of woe, my lamentations.

I was completely unaware, nor could I ever have imagined that such horrifying cruelty, such savage brutality could be inflicted on a young innocent girl with such depraved indifference. I speak here about personal calamity at the hands of the devil himself. Perhaps only an expert psychologist can understand my humiliating degradation, my paralyzing depression, the depth of my despair. My tragedy, or perhaps my preordained destiny, however insignificant in the eyes of this merciless world, deserves some explanation, some acknowledgement, some understanding, some philosophical discussion.

I want the world to know what happens to such a girl when she is plucked like a flower and then crushed and trampled upon without a moment's hesitation or thought. What happens to her? What about her shattered psyche, her mental anguish, her dejection? Her very soul is branded. She is trapped in a permanent dark maze where the danger of exposure lurks at every corner, where her memories like her shadow are always with her, ready to confront her at every turn. She burns in the towering inferno of hell from where she can never escape. I welcome the readers to my nightmare.

There were two happy events in our family, the first being my nikah ceremony, for which most of our extended family and friends had come from far and near. There was much revellry, jubilation and festivities, with all kinds of singing and dancing, and of course endless feasting on the most delicious of fares. It had been decided that my rukhsati (when I actually leave my parental abode and move in with my husband who so far, I had never set eyes on) was to take place after he finished his police training. He was a new recruit in the police department.

Soon after my nikah, the whole party of friends and family, along with the children and servants, were to travel by train to attend the wedding of my maternal uncle's daughter, who apart from being my cousin was a great friend and confidante of mine. On the day of the departure, our party of nearly forty or fifty people descended on the railway station. My mother, along with some other older ladies, was to travel in the second-class ladies' compartment. The rest of us, young girls and children, were to travel in the third-class compartment. There were about thirty of us altogether. The station was crowded, and between the overwhelming heat and the din of the vendors, the cries of the coolies carrying our luggage, and the general confusion, we were all quite exhausted even before we had begun our journey. We couldn't all find seats together, and so our party was split into two, half of us in one third-class ladies' compartment, and the other half in another. It was difficult to figure out who was sitting where. The train was crammed full but somehow I was lucky enough to find a seat in the corner, right next to the window.

My aunt gestured to me to come and sit next to her, but she was sitting in a very uncomfortable spot so I smiled and politely declined her offer. It was without doubt very boring and dull to be sitting alone without any interesting company, but I was content where I was. We had departed by the 12 noon train, and were to arrive at our destination at 11 pm. At the next station a crowd of peasant women got on board with their foul-smelling belongings and dirty children and as if this was not enough, at the third station another bridal party, with about two dozen women were stuffed into these two women's compartments. The result was such utter confusion that nobody could move or change places. I was at the other end, calmly sitting in a corner, my back resting against a pillow. Other women from the family were further ahead in another corner. My mother was in the second-class compartment while there were family members with me who were dull and uninteresting and I couldn't really have a conversation with them.

Exhausted by the day's events and stuffed like sardines in this small crowded train car, dealing with the shoving, pushing and unbridled, uncouth loud behaviour of the peasant women, sitting apart from everyone with nothing interesting going on, I felt as if I was in hell. I thanked God when the other bridal party departed at the next station. But my relief was short-lived because at the very next station another group of twice as many peasant women and chamarni's came barging in. I was so overwhelmed I could barely breathe.

I couldn't bear all the noise, the heat, and the stench that had permeated this compartment. It was giving me a headache. At dinnertime, first I refused all refreshments, then when parathas and other delicacies appeared before me, I realized I was hungry, started eating and ate too much. After such a delicious meal I started to feel drowsy. The sky had darkened, the heat had abated, I had opened the window and the air was cooler. The rocking movement of the train, along with the exhaustion of the day and the rich meal, made me drowsy and I started to nod off. I think I was awake until 10 o'clock, I'm quite sure I was awake and alert, but I found a little space to spread my legs and I finally fell into a deep, deep sleep. God have mercy. What was written in my destiny had to be, even in this way.

Life is nothing but a series of coincidences, sometimes one coincidence coming after another.

The first coincidence was that I fell into a deep sleep, the next one that the station which was my destination came on the opposite side from where I was seated, the third that my companions left without thinking about me. They left me behind like a useless piece of luggage. Finally, the last coincidence was that I was in such a sleep of death that waking up became impossible.

2

The Devil Within

I woke up to the sound of a harsh voice. Someone was shaking my shoulder roughly. For a moment I didn't know where I was. Enveloped in darkness I tried to peer at this person who was addressing me in a local peasant dialect. He was admonishing me loudly for sleeping in a train parked in the train yard. 'It is against the law to sleep in a parked train!' he shouted rudely.

My mind still in a fog, I sat up and tried to figure out where I was. He was standing over me, shouting, 'Get up! Get out! You can't sleep in a parked train carriage.'

I asked him what station we were at and on hearing his reply I realized that I had not only missed my station, but was now at the last station where the train line ended.

I quickly donned my burqa, gathered my wits, and started pleading with him to take me to the station master's residence. With a sinking heart I realized that not only was I very far from where I was supposed to be, but that I had no money. This man was part of the cleaning crew, a jamadar. After fuming and frothing for a bit, he calmed down after my frightened, cowering appeals, and softened. 'There are some members of your community (meaning, Muslims) that live on the other side.' I begged him to take me there. With a great deal of reluctance he agreed and I got off the train. I followed him. It was a dark, moonless night, I was following him across the criss-crossing train tracks, hissing engines and the bogies of parked trains. There were snake-like wires spread all around. I tripped and fell, scraping my knees and elbows, but quickly got up.

The inky darkness, the overcast sky without a single star looming above, the black veil of my burqa that covered my face, the steam from the engines—all seemed to be pointing ominously to an even more terrible scenario that awaited me. I glanced above. The harsh red light of the signal glared menacingly, it looked like a giant angry eye of the devil. Despite the heat I broke out in a cold sweat and accelerated my pace as I trudged behind the jamadar.

After going through many twists and turns, the jamadar brought me to a small dark house not far from the station. A grimy curtain hung on the door, the sight of which relieved me. There must be women inside, I surmised. The jamadar knocked on the door, a male voice answered and then a man opened the door. The jamadar told him my story. The man turned to me and courteously asked me to step inside. I lifted the curtain and entered through the door. The man stood outside talking to the jamadar.

I stood in shock as I came in through the door. It was a small, dark, airless house, with an inner courtyard with high walls. In front of the courtyard was a gloomy verandah with a low ceiling. A single room behind seemed ablaze with light. In the doorway to the room stood a man who was holding on to the door frame. There were no women in sight. I was filled with panic and my heart started to race.

I heard the door slam shut loudly behind me, as if to warn me that not only was there a man in front of me, but there was a man behind me. As the man who was behind me came forward after locking the door, fear gripped my heart. The thought rushing through my mind was '*Ya Allah! There is no one here except these two men.*' My throat turned dry and a sense of dread spread through my body. I tried my best not to lose my nerve.

The man who had closed the door behind me stepped forward and motioned me to sit on a charpoy in the verandah. Then the two men disappeared into the room in the front and shut the door. I could hear them talking to one another in low voices. I was trying to figure out what to do when the door opened and the two of them came out.

One of them held a brightly lit lantern in his hands. He held it up to my person and the two of them started examining me in the most impudent and insulting way. I stood still, wrapped in my burqa, while the two men stared at me as though trying to disrobe me with their eyes. I became alarmed and agitated. One of them turned to the other and said something in English. I couldn't understand what he said, but I was able to guess they were talking about my hands. I quickly tucked my hands inside the burqa.

Mustering up as much courage as I could, I tried to keep the tremour out of my voice and said with forced confidence, 'Please take me to the station and assist me in sending a wire to my family.'

The man who had opened the door took a step towards me, and said in a loud, rough manner, 'Who are you?'

I became more frightened and agitated and my words became jumbled. 'I want to leave this place.'

The second man then spoke to me in a softer, honeyed voice, in a most pleasant and conciliatory tone. 'Please don't worry. If you like we can both step outside to secure your peace of mind. The women will be back soon, there is no cause for alarm, we can call the women from across the street. Please go inside the room and close the door, we will get the women right away,'

Sensing my hesitation, he added, 'We are decent people, there is no need to fear us.' I felt a wave of embarrassment ripple through my body on hearing his words. 'We are decent people.' His tone was slightly sarcastic when he repeated this sentence. Frightened and feeling helpless, I moved towards the room and stepped in through the door. 'The women will be here soon, and we will send the wire right away,' he said reassuringly as he closed the door behind me.

3

A Terrifying Decision

I breathed a sigh of relief and looked around the room. There was a takht, a wooden settee, against one wall, two beds with covers on them, and one or two small tables. On the wall in front of me were two hooks with clothes hanging from them. I looked around again. There was no evidence suggesting the presence of women. I sat down on one of the beds. A storm was whirling around in my brain. Overcome by dread, I tried to calm my nerves. A sense of doom and gloom was coursing like fire through my veins. I tried to shake it off, but that feeling touched my very soul and I felt a chill as cold as death seize my heart.

'My God, what have I done? I should have never come to this room. I am making one mistake after another.'

I sat there as if frozen, trying to suppress these thoughts and calm my rapidly beating heart. I strained my ears to hear what was going on outside, but I could hear nothing except the lonely whistle of trains, the faint hissing of the steam and the distant clatter of trains running on the metal tracks. For a while I convinced myself there was no one outside, but I soon heard whispering sounds coming from behind the second door. That door had an empty charpoy leaning against it. I crept under this charpoy and placed my ear to the door. Uff! Oh my God! What I heard through that door froze the blood in my veins. Would that I had died before hearing such depraved filth. Those unforgettable words pierced through my ears and were etched in my very soul. The two men were conspiring together to inflict the most abominable, heinous, crime on my person. My virtue, my honour! My very physical integrity was in grave danger. They were discussing who or maybe both, should take part in this act to satisfy their despicable desires.

No woman, leave alone a sixteen-year-old innocent who had only lived in a most protected, chaste environment, in the strictest of purdah, should have to listen to the possibility of such an evil calamity like the one that was about to befall me. Every fibre in my body was trembling, I could hear the blood rushing through my ears as if a thousand snakes were hissing in unison, my breath was coming in short dry gasps, my heart was beating so hard it was ready to explode.

I felt the ground beneath my feet shaking, or was it my imagination? *'Is this really happening? Is this what my fate has in store for me? Does such degenerate immorality really exist? Man is believed to be cast in the image of God—are these two men cast in His image? Or are they the devil in disguise?'* I felt a swoon coming over me. *'Ya Allah! Was I to be a victim of such a profoundly cruel villainy?'*

I sat there like a sparrow, burrowing deep into her nest as a hawk approaches it. Listening against my will. Would that molten lead had been poured into my ears rendering me deaf! For an unmarried, sheltered girl to hear such disgusting talk, a discussion about defiling her honour, her violation with her own ears—perhaps this too was my fate.

The two rogues were having a most spirited discourse about what was in store for me. One of them had taken leave of all that is considered human and decent. He was the Devil Incarnate. He was saying that both would take advantage of this opportunity. He expressed himself assertively without any shame or decency. The other took a more measured and reasonable approach. He talked about what decency and decorum dictated in such a circumstance. I was dumbfounded—there were rules and regulations dictated by decency, decorum and the Scriptures for what they were about to inflict on me? He argued that once he had relations with me, I was categorically a sort of legal wife/woman of his, and that the religious rules relegated me illegal for his friend. He kept droning on and on about honesty, decency, religion, legality, all the while planning my ruination. That the other was in no mood to hear his arguments was plain and clear.

This hypocrisy was driving me mad and I was about to start screaming, when the first said to the other that even though he didn't agree with his friend's point of view, he was more than aware of his obligations as a host. He offered me to his guest as a gift, washing his hands off me. My fate was decided in such simple terms by these two nameless villains. I heard the decision with a sinking heart. I had been offered as a gift by the host to his guest. Such generosity, such hospitality! I thought bitterly.

4

The Devil At the Door

I heard the men get up and move away and I came out of the trance I was in. I crawled out from under the charpoy. I smelled danger all around me, my fate mirrored the darkness of the night. I looked desperately at the rock-hard, filthy walls, the low-hung ceiling. The offensive dank smell of the dungeon-like room seemed to crawl into my skin.

The unforgiving darkness enveloped me, the weak flickering flame of the lantern cast menacing shadows on those faded walls, the ghoulish dancing shadows mocked me, *'You can't escape. You are doomed. Your life is over! A terrifying future awaits you.'*

I saw a high window with closed shutters in one of the walls. I had previously not seen it. I climbed on top of the bed and flung the shutters open. The window opened into a dark alley at the back of the house. A sense of relief flooded over me. A few moments ago I had been in a state of panic, my heart hammering, my breath uneven and gasping, my body trembling. This window gave me a sense of confidence as I started to climb out of it with a newly regained vigour. The balmy air caressed my face, the darkness outside beckoned me, promising freedom. Just then, my outer clothing snagged on something and I bent down to unhook it.

A hand shot out of the dark room behind me, gripping my wrist in a steel vise. A bloodcurdling scream escaped from my lips as I was pulled back with such force that I lost my balance and tumbled onto the bed, landing on my back. Within a matter of seconds the man's hands were around my neck.

A low guttural growl so close to my ears that I could smell the stench of his breath, and then the words, 'Don't scream.' At the same time, he started to choke me. I was gasping for breath, trying to pry his hands off my neck, struggling underneath him as his elbow dug into my chest, muffled cries emanating from my lips. He stretched to close the shutters with one hand while trying to hold me down with the other. I kicked and struggled and managed to slip out of his grasp.

After slamming the window hurriedly, my tormentor turned to me. Taking a chance on my life, I darted quickly in front of him and grabbed a three-legged small table. I looked at him with murderous eyes. I was no longer afraid. I was full of rage and frenzy. I was ready to kill or be killed.

I lifted the table above my head and screamed, 'You villain! You rogue! Get away from me, don't you dare take a step towards me. I will split your head in two.'

Seeing my bravado he paused, appearing somewhat unsure of himself. 'Your screaming and shouting will be in vain,' he retorted. I glowered at him; a storm of fury was swirling in my chest. I snapped back at him with contempt and disgust. 'Coward! Low life! Who is shouting? Who is screaming? Are you dreaming? I will bash your brain to mush! Who do you think you are?' Emboldened once more, he shook his head in disbelief and said, 'I can tell you won't listen to reason.' With that he moved towards me.

'Don't you dare!' I shouted, and lifted the table higher above my head. With the speed of a striking viper he was upon me. Holding the table firmly with both hands I struck him on the head. He tried to protect himself by raising a hand to ward off the blow, but he was too late. The table hit his forehead with full force. His knees buckled and he fell face forward in slow motion. I was still standing on the bed with the table in my hands. Blood was pouring out of his forehead. He tried to get up and with great difficulty raised himself to his knees, and then collapsed on his side with a groan.

I felt queasy, all that blood, that was fast accumulating on the floor frightened me. A shiver of disbelief and disgust passed through my body.

'I have killed him!' My heart sank as this thought raced through my mind. He lay there, lifeless, shallow breaths emanating from his open mouth. 'What should I do?' I thought. I sat down on the bed and bent down to look at him. *'He is merely unconscious not dead,'* I reassured myself. *'This is another opportunity for me to escape.'* I moved to the window once more, still shaken by this violent encounter.

His breathing was becoming more laboured, punctuated with periods when he was not breathing at all. He gasped and appeared to be choking on something. I stopped and looked back; he was really struggling to breathe. His breath became more erratic, shallow and slow. The pool of blood around his head, that raspy breath, his listless body. *'He is dying! I have killed him!'* The thought that I had killed him overwhelmed me, I got off the bed to confirm that he wasn't really dead or dying. He appeared to have stopped breathing. I bent down to get a better look.

That was the mistake of my life. I will always regret it. It was a diabolical ploy on his part. He leapt up, his hands coiled around my neck like a python, and he began choking me to death, but not before I had bit his finger as hard as I could. He pinned me down with his weight, with one hand he was choking me, while stuffing my chador into my mouth with the other. I thrashed my head wildly from left to right, I clenched my teeth and closed my mouth tightly, but his fingers dug into my cheeks with such force that he was able to pry my mouth open. He started to stuff the chador in my mouth roughly. I couldn't breathe. I started to gag, but he paid no attention.

After stuffing the cloth in my mouth, he held my hands in his strong hands and shook me so hard my teeth rattled.

'I will kill you,' he growled. 'If you so much as make a peep, I will choke you to death.' He shook his clenched fist in my face. He then released my wrist and scowled at me, an expression of rage taking hold of his face.

I was gagging and choking and despite his threat I lifted my hands towards my face to relieve my agony. Before my hands could reach my face, he slapped me with the speed of lightning on my temple with such force that I fell. I lay there on my side, my face stinging with that hard slap, my ears ringing, my head swimming. With weak and trembling hands and great difficulty I pulled myself up into a sitting position. I now realized what brute force and physical abuse was about. I took a good look at my tormentor, my assailant. He was about twenty-two to twenty-three years of age, tall, of muscular build. He was fair-skinned, with good features, a wide forehead, and large, exceptionally bright eyes. His thin lips were curled in a snarl. And the overall expression was that of a man who uses force to get his way. I lowered my head and joined my hands in supplication. Tears of pain, humiliation, and fear were running down my cheeks, I couldn't breathe and waves of nausea were rising up in my throat. I started to retch. I motioned with my hands if I could remove the chador that was gagging me. He nodded, threatening me once again.

'If you make the slightest noise, I will choke you to death.' Then he pulled a knife out and said, 'I will butcher you if you make the smallest sound. No one can hear your screams and shouts. Swear you won't scream.' I nodded. He once again flashed the knife at my face and removed the gag from my mouth.

'Don't be afraid,' he said gently. 'I won't hurt you.'

As soon as he removed the gag from my mouth, I collapsed. I was sobbing hysterically. I had covered my face with my chador, with my hands folded like a beggar. I implored him to let me go. 'Please let me go, I beg of you!' I whimpered. 'In the name of God, please release me.'

'Don't worry,' he said in a softer tone, as he wiped the blood oozing from his forehead. 'I will not hurt you.' He offered me water. 'Here rinse your mouth and drink some cold water, you will feel better.'

I did as I was told.

'Sit down like a human being, I want to talk to you,'

he said. After drinking the water I felt somewhat revived. I covered my face with my chador and started weeping again, begging for mercy.

'What is your name? Who are you?' he inquired.

I looked at him from the corner of my eye, as my face was hidden with my chador, wondering what this line of questions was about.

'What is your father's name?' he asked next.

The thought raced through my mind that whether he knows my name or not, he plans to dishonour me. If I tell him my name, or my father's name, he will later on shame and blackmail me. I remained silent. I didn't want my parents to be disgraced. If he violates me, I will kill myself, I thought. Nobody would know who I was, I would just be a nameless dead girl. No need to blacken my father and mother's face.

Observing my silence, he asked, 'Are you married?' I looked at him carefully with one exposed eye. He asked me again if I was married. I thought about it for a while, not wishing to expose my husband to the risk of embarrassment on account of what seemed to be my inevitable fate. I shook my head in the negative.

'Which city do you hail from?' he asked. He was becoming irritated by my silence. 'Where do you want to go?'

I hastily informed him about my destination, and then

I again started to plead with him. 'For God's sake let me go, please take me where I want to go.'

This was the prelude to the catastrophe that was to befall me. I was now in the grip of the devil himself. The villainous brute started to use his animal cunning, and began to flirt with me, with cheap and trite dialogue, uttering clichéd declarations of love and affection that belonged on the pages of third-class novels. Those disgusting vulgar words pierced into my heart like spears, those hackneyed banal metaphors resounded and reverberated in my head like a hammer on an anvil. The flush on my cheeks was not a blush, but redness brought on by shame and anger. The perspiration of embarrassment broke out on my forehead. This was neither love nor romance, this was abasement. Is this my fate? I wondered. To be raped like an animal in this filthy dungeon with its white crypt. I sat there with my head lowered in shame at my unimaginable situation, weeping, begging, beseeching, trying my best to move the devil's cold heart.

I want the readers of my letter to fully understand my predicament. A young innocent girl, or for that matter any young woman, who is engaged, or has had a nikah, starts looking forward to an imaginary world. A world full of trust and love, laughter and joy, a safe and secure home, where she basks in the warm affection of her spouse. She looks at the world, which is part of her imagination and desires, with joy, contentment and satisfaction, and yes, with absolute confidence. All this was mine until a few hours ago. A few hours ago, I was a newly married (though only in name) young girl, contemplating a life full of happiness and wonder, of new experiences and adventure, and all that had been snatched away from me by this unknown demon who wore the mask of a human being.

I was thinking that if I wasn't already married, I would have made a compromise and accepted this savage beast. I would have somehow convinced him that if he was so desirous of me, then he should get two witnesses and a maulvi. But my position was different. I already belonged to someone else. I was at a loss as to how to save myself from the clutches of this animal. On my begging and pleading he promised to marry me. In short, he was promising to go through a nikah in the morning if I obliged him. I on the other hand was playing my hand by insisting that he get a maulvi right away now knowing full well that the promise of a nikah was nothing but a ploy, but he too was well aware that my insistence for a speedy nikah was a ploy to buy time.

I was firm in my decision not to oblige him, he was determined to have his way. His sickening, honeyed flattery fell on deaf ears, his persuasive promises and attempts to soften me were met with a firm and later on, harsh refusal. Infuriated and humiliated, and unable to cajole me to do his bidding, he pounced on me and after felling me to the floor started choking me again, slapping and punching me at the same time. My hands were free and the knife he had used to threaten me lay within reach. I grabbed it and tried to attack him, but a sixteen-year-old girl was no match for this muscular maniac. He wrested the knife from my hand and threw it across the room. He continued hitting me and stuffed my chador into my mouth again. He tied my hands behind my back. His behaviour became wilder and frenzied and my innocence and femininity were crushed by brute force.

I could do nothing but bang my head on the floor. I wanted to die, I thought I could do so by banging my head against the floor with all my might. I was being choked and beaten, I could barely breathe, my determination to kill myself grew stronger. I banged my head so hard on the stone floor that I passed out. When I woke up, I realized I was in the devil's embrace. My life as I knew it was ruined. A pathetic whimper escaped my lips and I fainted again.

5

Ruination

'Fear the Sigh of the Oppressed
For Their Prayers Are Answered By God Himself.'

Oppressor!

Uff! That word 'oppressor'! What a formidable, terrifying word. And the Oppressor himself? A grotesque, frightening, three-eyed, fire-breathing giant, emitting an earth-shaking roar of evil and villainy that destroys everything in its path, like a dragon breathing fire, burning everything that comes in its path to a cinder. A monumental monster composed of everything that is foul, putrid, offensive, loathsome.

The Oppressor, drunk on his all-powerful stature of

obscenity and defilement, covered with slime and excrement, dancing his devil's dance, after the commencement of a terrifying abomination. Indeed, this oppression, violation, are the most heinous of all human crimes. The light of the world is extinguished when immorality and savagery hand a young girl into the bloody talons of an oppressor. It appears as if the light of Ahura Mazda, the God of fire, sunlight, and life has been thrown into darkness by Ahriman, the Lord of darkness and death. But that did not occur, the world with all its glory revolved at the same speed, the sun and the moon and the stars followed their prescribed paths, the weak remained oppressed, the oppressor remained victorious with all his power and pride. Nothing changed. Nothing at all. It was as if this monstrous crime had not taken place.

In actuality this crime and its consequences were mine to suffer alone. My universe changed. My life changed. I was no more what I once was, but the world remained the same, though not for me. The loss of my honour, my chastity, altered me forever. I became a burden on this world, a disgrace and dishonour to my family, and to my husband. But the oppressor who inflicted this torture on me? He remains untainted, unburdened, unshackled; his devilish behaviour does not change his life. I was the sacrifice for the Lord of Darkness.

My honour and respect were the sacrifice in his temple of evil, a devotee of the devil wanted to pay homage to the Lord of Darkness and I was chosen. I saw that what was putrid and foul had overcome purity and decency. Innocence was lynched as it kicked and screamed, and the dead corpse of everything that was good and noble was being torn apart by the vulture's talons, its flesh was swollen with maggots, dogs were fighting over its fresh bones, it wasn't just me weeping—decency, humanity, innocence, purity and nobility of man were all mourning the death of their honour. If every honourable, virtuous maiden is the symbol of Islam, then every savage oppressor is Yazid, that abominable Yazid who tried to rape and dishonour Islam at Karbala. He gripped Islam by the throat, his bloody hands determined to disgrace and destroy it. The prophecy of Imam Hussain was fulfilled, and the savage killing of the Imam, the blood of Hussain and thus the blood of the prophet of Islam was spilled in the desert at Karbala. That noble blood retained the prestige and honour of Islam. We see that Islam still has its purity and chastity, but Islam has been weeping tears of blood since that fateful day 1,400 years ago. But, but—my sighs, my cries—my tears! All remained unanswered. That I should be so abandoned in my hour of need, was not possible. But I had to face bitter reality. No earthshaking event took place when I was brutalized. No heavenly intervention came in the face of my tragedy. My world from now onwards would be full of pain and misery, just as the tragedy of Karbala, despite Yazid's failure to destroy Islam, still remains a constant source of pain and sorrow for the Islamic world. The loss of a poor, innocent girl's honour is not just equal to the tragedy of Karbala, but is worse, for her friends, family and for herself. It too, is a constant source of sorrow. It is a constant pain, a reminder, a disgrace and shame that is remembered for seven generations to come, and more.

That poor girl, and her family, cannot rest in peace even in death, for people point to her very grave and say, this is where that poor girl who was raped is buried. It is as if the whole family is suffering from leprosy, as if their faces are blackened with shame forever. It is in moments like this that justice itself cries out loudly, saying, societal rules are not just harsh, but cruel and oppressive.

And the brute that has committed this savagery? His face? His face beaming with satisfaction and contentment, the smug self-congratulatory expression, his heart filled with the satisfaction of his animal lust, he appears drunk on his success, he looks at the world with great joy and gratification like a fly on the sweets in a sweetshop, thinking, 'This world full of delicacies belongs to Me! This is all for me! This is all prepared for me!'

And I? I was thinking about what I was before and what I am now. Was I created just for this unfortunate day when at the height of my youth, beauty and innocence, I was to become the target of such cruelty, such brutality? Was I born to be like a rose that is plucked from its stem to be thrown carelessly on a plague-ridden corpse instead of being woven into a garland that adorns a victor? I was waiting for the ground to split open or the sky to fall down, but none of this happened, and I was still in arms of the devil. I was looking at this savage beast that had destroyed my life.

I was sitting on the bed weeping over my fate. My future. What happens next? Where will I go now? How can I face the world? Yes, death is the only answer! I wept loudly and bitterly at my ruination, and my oppressor appeared proud and satisfied, plying me with his undying love, his false promises. I was overwhelmed by disgust. The sun rose to a new dark day for me. He packed his bags and with a final goodbye beat a hasty retreat.

After he left, the other man, the so-called host, came. He reassured me that my secret was safe. I heard these words and to my own horror remained silent and alive. I should have died with shame. I was being reassured of secrecy, and I was sitting there calmly, listening to him. I was conspiring with the man who sold me to be abused by his guest. He shook my shoulder and asked me to accompany him to the station. Wrapped in my burqa I followed him. Like a walking corpse. On arriving at the station, I was informed by the station master that there was a telegram from my brother. He had not mentioned it before and now after reading the telegram I found out my brother was on his way to get me. I sat in the waiting room weeping at my fate.

6

A Story of the Past

Bhai Sahib was arriving by the 8 a.m. train. It was now 7:30 a.m., I was sitting in the ladies' waiting room at the railway station. A future as dark as death awaited me. The pressing thought at that moment was that Bhai Sahib will be here soon, what will he say when he finds out? As if I will tell him all that had happened! I thought bitterly.

The man, the station master in whose house I had spent that fateful night, came back to me again, and said in a confidential whisper, 'For God's sake don't tell anyone what happened.' He took a few steps to leave, then came back again, bent over my seated figure and whispered further instructions. 'Tell your brother you had a most comfortable night with the women in my home.'

He left and I was thinking, how can I tell my brother what happened? What words can I possibly use to describe what happened to me? But I can't lie to my brother either. I can't deceive him. I thought about it some more. I decided I won't say anything, I will remain silent. Burdened with these thoughts, I wept bitterly.

Bhai Sahib came, hugged me, with what love and concern he inquired after my health and then, instead of remaining silent as I had decided, I started to conspire with my tormentors. I was shocked and horrified with my own deceit and cunning. I hastened to inform my brother that I had spent a most comfortable night with the women in the station master's house. I said what I had been instructed to say.

He was worried about my appearance. I didn't tell him I had been beaten and abused. I lied brazenly and blamed a fall, exhaustion, and anxiety for my appearance. He admonished me about sleeping so soundly, and I who had been known for my honesty, started lying again about how kind the women in the station master's house were, how just to appease me they asked the men to leave the house, and so on. My lies! My deceit! My falsehood surprised and disgusted my own self. Bhai Sahib said that he should go and thank the station master for his kindness towards me.

'Maybe I should reward him?' I didn't know how to stop him. He went to the station master, and my heart sank. Oh woe! He was thanking this monster! I couldn't bear it and a fresh storm of weeping ensued. Through a veil of tears, I saw my brother standing next to the station master, puffing at his cigarette, smiling and thanking him. He stood there with the pride and confidence of his status and class. If only he knew what had really happened. As for the station master, he stood beside him, smirking slyly. How my loyalties had shifted from my own brother to my abuser. It was as if that monster owned me. Like a puppet on a string, I had parroted what he coached me to say. The scene with my trusting brother and the station master cut straight into my heart.

My abuser had written his name and address on a piece of paper and pushed it with two fingers into my waistcoat pocket. I tore it into shreds and crushed it beneath my feet. Maybe I should have kept that piece of paper. I should not have thrown it away. Now I was remembering his conversations that had been full of love and affection. I felt if somehow my nikah could be annulled, or if I were to be divorced, then I could become his. I should be handed over to my abuser.

I would say to him, 'You monster, you have ruined my life, I can no longer be with anyone else. You have to pick me up from where I have fallen and keep me as your wife.' I deserved him. I was damaged, disgraced and discarded, fit only for that. I was useless for this world. I didn't want to go home. I wanted to either die, or have my nikah annulled and to be with the man who had abused and destroyed me. But that was not possible now. I didn't even know his name. I didn't have his address. I have made another mistake, I thought.

I was still ruminating about all the mistakes I had made when the train with its ear-splitting, screaming whistles and ground-shaking, metallic clatter, pulled into the station, billowing dark clouds of smoke, as if laughing at and ridiculing my fate. Bhai Sahib helped me into the ladies' compartment. I sat in the corner next to the window with my face covered, crying silently. There were only a handful of women in the compartment. I was too embarrassed to look them in the eye. These happy, content, decent women, they had no idea about what I had become, they saw me as one of them, when the reality was completely different. They had no idea about my ordeal.

The journey was short and within the blink of an eye we had reached our destination. When I arrived at my uncle's house, everyone was delighted to see me alive and well. The house was bursting at the seams with joy and happiness at the forthcoming wedding of my cousin. Meanwhile all I wanted was to be left alone, left alone to lick my wounds and weep hysterically over the catastrophe that had befallen me. On the way to my uncle's house, I had decided that I must share my ordeal, my tragedy, with someone.

I was closest to the bride-to-be, my cousin. I had decided she would be my confidante, my pillar of strength and understanding in my grief, but now I realized that it was impossible. She was constantly surrounded by a crowd of happy young women. Alas! Once I would have been one of these women, laughing, singing, teasing, joking. Very soon everyone noticed my lack of spirit, my sad demeanour and started to inquire about it. At first I was able to deflect their attention by claiming exhaustion from the journey, the worry of being lost. My distraught state, however, was so noticeable and seemed so out of proportion to my explanation that it piqued the curiosity and concern of those around me. They started pressing me for information, insisting that I tell them the real reason. I kept protesting, saying that I was just shaken up by the whole experience. Finally, after some self-examination, I realized that indeed my appearance and manner had changed so drastically that no one would believe me.

My cousin asked me several times personally, and despite repeating again and again that scripted lie that I had stuck to from the beginning, she started to argue with me.

'What kind of travel exhaustion is this that it just doesn't seem to leave you? It's not just that you have forgotten how to sing and laugh, you appear frightened, tell me what is really the issue here?'

I managed somehow to calm her down for a short while, but she didn't quite believe me. Finding an opportune moment, she once again started to tangle with me.

'I'm convinced something's happened to you. You're not revealing the whole truth. Did you fall in love with someone?'

I became incensed. 'You wretch!' I retorted. 'May your tongue catch fire, you're dressed as a modest, virtuous bride and yet your tongue keeps wagging.' In short, I scolded her severely, but my denials were useless, my face belied my words, and no one believed me.

They all surrounded me, clamouring for further explanations. I had to hear such comments as, 'She has lost her spark!' 'She doesn't talk or laugh anymore!' 'She seems lost!'

'Why this stunned silence?' 'What has happened to her?' And on and on they went. The people around me were making my life miserable. This constant inquisition was making me lose my mind. My patience had reached a breaking point and I began to lose my temper. I gave a few of them such a tongue-lashing that I silenced them. But in reality, none of this made any difference. People around me sensed that something more than what I had offered them had happened. I was consumed by my sorrow. The joy and celebration of the wedding seemed artificial and contrived to me. You can imagine my own hypocritical participation. I was relieved when we returned home. I would have some relief from the constant badgering and questioning, I thought, and felt a great burden lift from my shoulders. I was convinced that I would find the peace and quiet my heart desired. Perhaps I would be able to reflect upon the future. But I found my life to be as painful as before. The story of my getting lost in the train had reached my hometown. And the women started to whisper about me and look at me suspiciously. A few of them began to ask pointed questions.

I finally became convinced that my outward look and behaviour had changed so drastically that anyone who had known me before noticed the difference immediately, and became concerned about me. I started putting on an act with false smiles, laughter and gaiety, maintaining a constant chatter about silly things. I was trying my best to forget, and made an effort to pretend that nothing had happened. I became quite successful at this, I hardened my heart and tried to convince myself that whatever had happened in the past, I should do my best to forget it.

In order to distract myself, I turned to my friend Arifa. I invited her over six or seven times, and often went to see her also. After returning from a visit with her one day I became ill and was very sick after that for several days. I was suffering from headaches, fever and chills. I thought I was dying and for the time being I forgot all about my ordeal. When I got up from my sickbed, I realized I was not as obsessed with what had happened. It seemed I was in the process of forgetting, some of the pain and horror slowly began fading away. After some time, I felt I had almost forgotten the incident, or rather put it in the past ... a warning!

PART TWO

7

Prelude to Disaster

I toiled diligently to put my dreadful experience behind me, and the result was that I managed to completely forget it or as completely as one could. My crime was invisible. I will call it my crime as I was trying my very best to conceal it by not sharing my unfortunate experience with anyone. Certainly I didn't want anyone to find out.

There was a sheet of silence that lay over my dark deeds, my sorrow was no longer as fresh as before. But my conscience pricked me constantly. *'How are you going to face your husband? How will you look into his eyes?'* That same conscience had now gone to sleep. No! No, it wasn't just asleep, it was formulating plans for deceit and cunning and such plans that my husband and even his father, wouldn't be able to figure out if these pearls were real or artificial.

There was a time when I used to entertain the thought that I would narrate the whole story to him, my husband. After all, isn't the relationship between a husband and wife supposed to be the closest in the world? I would weep and cry and reveal to him all my suffering. I would show him that I was innocent, a victim of extreme cruelty, that I had not transgressed, that I was not a sinner. Perhaps he would accept my apology, perhaps his tender heart would be merciful and he would forgive and accept me.

No! No! I am innocent, my heart is pure, I was not responsible, I was not at fault.

But now these thoughts had long left my mind. I planned to keep this dark secret from my husband just like I had concealed it from everyone else. After all, I was innocent, I am innocent, the sin is not mine. I should be able to meet my husband without hesitation, to look into his eyes without blinking with shame. It was the truth. I was not to blame, so why start life with a discussion about this painful chapter. I firmly decided that's what I would do. I had somehow suffered in silence, and had almost convinced myself to forget that incident when suddenly something entirely different came to light.

I was in complete denial when this dark, ugly, ominous cloud of suspicion arose and an unbelievable dread of doubt cast a shadow over my already distressed life. For a young woman to notice an irregularity in her bodily function is not unusual, I reasoned with myself. But after what had transpired, obviously I was going to worry and be wary. I was afraid that this might mean something else. I sat down and tried to calculate. After counting the number of days, I became more concerned and scared, but I was still in denial and convinced myself by deliberately miscalculating. Then I decided to share my concerns with Arifa, to tell her all that had transpired. I went to her home just for that purpose, but somehow the opportunity to talk didn't present itself and all my plans and fretting proved futile. Then, in five or six days the worry along with the concern completely left me. After careful inquiry I reached the conclusion that this irregularity happened sometimes and there was no need for alarm. This explanation satisfied me. I allowed myself to be convinced that everything was fine. Days passed, weeks passed, I was laughing at my own fears, my foolishness. This was all just my imagination. My disbelief was complete.

However, a time came when I had to face reality. This was not just a suspicion or my imagination. I became frantic. *'Oh my God, what am I to do?'*

Every passing day seemed like a mountain that had to be climbed. I was no longer doubtful or unsure. I knew deep in my heart that my fears were not unfounded. It was the truth, all the signs and symptoms pointed towards it. God was not willing to allow me my little secret. The curtain of lies was going to be torn apart. I would have to face judgment and abasement, now I would be truly shamed and disgraced! I would have to reveal everything and to everyone. Mother, brother, sisters, friends, family! I was destroyed for this world and for my faith, my beliefs. Everyone would know.

This was my fate, my preordained fate which was written in the blackest of ink and it flashed before my eyes. These frightening deadly facts! My honour, my reputation. My self-respect. All laid bare like a corpse for everyone to see, while carrion-eating vultures and birds of prey were circling above and slowly descending to partake of this corpse.

I was shocked, stunned. In constant fear. *'Oh my God! What's going to happen next? What sin did I commit that I'm being punished so? Is the kingdom of God really this helpless? Does innocence have to be punished so? This punishment that I am getting now I do not deserve!'* These thoughts raced through my mind, crowded my mind, they never left me. I was crushed and overwhelmed by my obsessive thoughts. These thoughts were killing me, they were finding new ways to torture me.

A myriad contemplations and scenarios ran through my mind, frightening me, torturing me. I kept obsessing about all that could happen to me now.

When my father finds out how his darling daughter has suffered, what will he do?

Will he kill himself? Will he shoot himself with a pistol?

And if he doesn't do that, would his friends, neighbours, come feigning sympathy, but in reality, out of curiosity? Will they want to know who this beast was? Who was this monster?

What was done to your daughter?

What did he do?

And when my brother finds out?

Oh my God, what will he do out of anger and pride?

I will not be surprised if he kills me and then takes his own life.

The whole neighbourhood will gossip.

And what of my poor mother?

The neighbourhood women will pretend to be sympathetic but in reality, would be there just for titillation.

And those who are jealous of us?

Our hidden enemies?

They will exaggerate all that has happened.

Such thoughts chased one after another, they were so painful that I actually screamed! I now realized that there was only one solution, there was only one choice. Death! Death was the only choice, the only solution I had. Death would solve all these problems, there was no other choice.

After contemplating about it for quite a while I decided that I would drown myself in the well in our inner courtyard. I firmly resolved that I would throw myself in this well, finish my life and thus save my father and grandfather's honour, and prevent their disgrace. I spent many hours coming up with this plan. I was now convinced that this was really the best strategy.

People most probably would say that I fell in accidentally and then the whole scandal would drown just like me. I consoled myself and became quite satisfied with my plan. I decided that I should take a look at this well. I climbed on to the ledge and peeped inside. It was dark, it was deep enough and after peering into it I could see the sinister movement in the dark waters below, beckoning me with their imaginary soft, lapping sound. When I thought about the depth of the well, I quaked, my heart trembled. I quickly drank some sweet water from the well and stepped back.

The night was silent. A dark night darker than my fate surrounded me. The silence of the terrifying darkness pierced by the light of the stars, appeared ominous. The twinkling stars seemed like spears aimed at me. We all slept outside in the courtyard. I sat up in my bed and looked around. All was quiet. I looked at my mother's bed and listened to her breathing. Other than the chirping of the cicadas there was silence everywhere. This is the right moment, I thought. I got up quietly and approached the well.

I climbed on the ledge of the well with a heavy and reluctant heart and looked up at the dark, silent sky one last time. I saw a shooting star that seemed to be aiming straight at me. It burned brightly but after a while its lights dimmed and disappeared and it plunged into the blackness of the sky. I thought, I'm like that shooting star, I was planning to drown the light of my life, the brightness of my youth in that deep, dark well. With a great deal of effort, I peered inside the well. Looking into this deep tunnel was like looking at the Day of Judgement. I didn't see a well, but instead a frightening, monstrous colossal python that darted towards me with its mouth wide open. It was such a terrifying experience that it was only by a miracle that I did not scream and fall into its jaws. I forgot all about drowning myself and turned around and ran back like a mad woman, convinced that this python was following me. I ran as fast as I could and within a blink of an eye, I was leaning against one of the pillars of the verandah, panting and gasping for breath. My heart was beating violently, my eyes staring at the well as I became convinced that the monstrous python was coming towards me, to swallow me. After a while I calmed down. I was defeated. Forget about jumping into the well, I thought, I could not even look into it.

All the while I knew that death was the only path that was left for me to take. I decided to undo the jute rope from my charpoy, and making a loop, I put it around my neck and pulled it. The choking sensation overwhelmed me and I was unable to bear it. I realized that difficult as it was to live, killing myself was even more difficult. I lay down in bed thinking, if only I could obtain some poison. Arsenic would be perfect, I thought. I kept thinking about it and then I fell asleep.

I was dreaming. It was a dreadful nightmare. In my nightmare I saw the well. It was like a black monster that was yawning and as it yawned and inhaled, I was propelled forward towards its gaping, cavernous mouth. I was tumbling like dried leaves in a strong wind, swirling around helplessly with each breath of this monster. I became so frightened that I held on tightly to the corners of my bed. I felt as if the well with its wide-open mouth was trying to swallow me. I kept holding on fast to my bed and screamed hysterically. My mother woke up and when she came to me it took me a while to figure out what was going on. I told her I had had a frightening nightmare.

The next day when I awoke, for a while it seemed that my problems would be solved. My mind seemed to be somewhat at ease. But then very soon all of those ideas and thoughts returned obsessively. My mind was coming up with a new solution every minute and then discarding it just as fast. Once again, I started to think about the big mistake I had made in throwing away my assailant's address and name that he had given me. Oh my God! When my secret is revealed and my in-laws find out, what will happen then? Would I be divorced? I would be like the dhobi's dog, a dog that belongs neither at home nor at the workplace. Ahh! if only

I had kept that address. If I had known this was going to happen to me, I would have kept his name and address, and when confronted with this monumental problem, I would have been able to contact him. My thoughts kept obsessing about finding him, of somehow developing wings to fly to him, and say to him, you monster, you savage beast, you have destroyed my life. You are responsible for my tortured life, this life which is worse than death, you are responsible for this hell I am living in, you have to come up with a solution. I would not even entertain the idea, the thought that he might deny my request, that he may laugh and walk away from it all. He cannot, he cannot walk away from this, he has to acknowledge his crime. He has to save me.

But what was the point of thinking these useless thoughts. I didn't even know the name of the station master. This storm of thoughts, this continuous obsession, this constant pain that surrounded me, was choking me, killing me. I tried my best to stop this obsession and think about what I should do next.

8

The Beauty of Virtue

I knew now that I would not be able to conceal my predicament any longer. The curtain of silence and secrecy was going to be shredded soon. If not now, then in a couple more months, the entire incident would come to light. My black deeds, my desire to conceal this incident, would be torn asunder.

So, the question now was that if I could not maintain the secrecy for long, why didn't I just go and reveal it as soon as I could to my friend Arifa? After a great deal of reflection I decided that I would tell her my secret. I thought about it several times and then arrived at Arifa's the very next day.

As soon as she saw me, she was able to figure out that something was the matter. She said, 'Dear sister! You appear to be really troubled, what is the matter? Is everything all right?'

I sat down and instead of answering her, I looked at her carefully. She was a virtuous, unmarried maiden. Decency was visible in her innocent eyes! Chastity gently kissed her noble forehead. The glowing aura of purity surrounded her and was reflected on her face. She had all that was desirable in a maiden and I—Oh woe! I was nothing but a crushed and soiled young woman.

I was a flower that had been plucked before it could bloom and had been trampled upon in such a way that every petal had been bruised and lost its sweet fragrance. I was revolted by my own person, I could not tolerate the foul smell that emitted from my destroyed youth. I was embarrassed by my own existence, I personified sin itself, trouble itself. On the outside I looked the same, but my inner self, my grotesque inner, present self was an acknowledgement and revelation that evil and the Devil existed, and yet by God I was innocent.

There is a light which surrounds a virtuous maiden and the beauty of that light shines like a star on the noble forehead of the immaculate maiden. I saw it on Arifa. The light that illuminates you with its beauty was hers, and on my unlucky forehead, I bore the black mark of the devil. Whereas Arifa was a statue of light, I represented the darkness of evil.

Instead of answering her, I was looking at her as these thoughts were running through my mind. As I looked at her, my heart became overwhelmed, my eyes started to tear, I put my arms around her spontaneously and hugged her and started to weep at the same time. My grief poured out of me like a river.

On seeing my distress, she became frightened and agitated. In a trembling voice she said, 'My dear sister,' and then very gently, she extricated herself from my arms. I saw tears of sympathy hanging on her eyelashes 'Oh my God, dear sister, what happened?'

My answers were accompanied by my tears, I told her my story between sobbing and weeping; I felt as if my heart was breaking, I poured out all that had happened, somehow I revealed all my secrets to her, from the beginning to the end. I narrated how that monster caught me, how I fought for my life, how despite all my attempts he overcame me, and since then I had been hiding that whole sordid incident like cats hide their excrement. Now by a cruel twist of fate, by the will of God, everything would be revealed to everyone.

While I was narrating the story, I was also looking at her face and saw the terrifying effect it had on her. She listened to my ordeal in complete silence, in shock. I looked deep into her beautiful eyes to see whether they were showing the light of compassion, or the darkness of disgust. And I saw! I saw that her beautiful eyes that were filled with compassion only a moment ago, were now dripping with the darkness of disgust and revulsion.

My heart sank and I burst out in tears again. I said, 'Dear sister! I know I'm worthy of hate, disgust and revulsion, but please, for God's sake please, realize I'm a victim, a victim of my fate. It is my fate that led me to this dark space. I may be worthy of your anger, your disgust, but I'm also worthy of some mercy, if you turn your eyes away from me, how will I live then?'

On hearing my anguished cry, her expression changed, she was once again full of love and solace. She started to weep, the flood of mercy wiped the blackness of hatred away. She was sympathetic to me, her empathy towards me was real, that disgust that I had seen in her eyes, was perhaps a natural phenomenon, that any person who was pure and noble would feel towards such a heinous act. An honourable, respectable, pure nature is extremely sensitive. And this sensitivity makes it turn its face away from ugliness.

Arifa had never heard of such an incident, how could she bear the weight of my tragedy? As it is innocence and pure feminine instinct is so delicate that it finds even a discussion about this kind of an incident an assault on its own self. An unmarried maiden has the sweet scent of virtue about her and in her presence, forget about the discussion of my loss of honour, even my very breath was an insult to her innocence and purity.

Arifa looked at me with frightened, sympathetic eyes that were filled with tears, she blinked nervously, her lips trembled. This was probably the worst incident that could happen to a young girl's best friend. There was no doubt now that this dark secret would soon come to light. At the most it could be hidden for another month or two. The question now was, what was to be done. Arifa, the poor innocent, what could she do? She sat there quietly with a sad and frightened look on her face.

This is such a dark and hideous and unnatural tale that all women, regardless of their differences, friends, family or neighbours would be shocked, stunned in disbelief if they hear it. They would sit there with sober expressions on their faces, as if someone had died. That was how Arifa looked at me now, and I looked at her apologetically, as a victim of such a crime does, guilty, responsible, ashamed. This indeed was a fate worse than death.

I looked at Arifa's quiet content fate. Perhaps she was thinking about how helpless we both were. It is worth reflecting upon the cruel and merciless laws of society if a young woman becomes a victim of a man's lust. She is herself forced to remain silent, to keep this crime hidden.

The question is, why is it so? Why can't she openly reveal what she has suffered? Why does she, the victim, have to hide the crime committed by someone else and on her person? Why can't she tear this cruelty that she is hiding in her heart away from herself and throw it in the public domain? Why can't she throw the criminal in the arena of public opinion and expose him for society to judge him? But she can't do this, can she?

She's helpless, because if she dares to stand up and point a finger at her oppressor and narrate her sufferings, society will turn on her. People will forget all about the criminal and the crime will be all hers. She will be punished severely; she will be cast aside like used goods. Society will brand her forehead with a red-hot branding iron. It would be made clear to her that she does not belong in the society of decent women, those decent women who have been fortunate and not been the victim of an evil, lustful man. She would be ostracized, isolated, she could never expect to be married or have any man look at her with respect or with intentions of marriage. Society and family would like to cut her off like a cancer and throw her in a garbage dump. This is what our law-abiding society doles out as punishment to an innocent victim.

A woman who has been ravaged is forced to hide it as though it were her crime, hoping for the Day of Judgement when justice will finally prevail, when the persecutor, the oppressor, the tyrant will be meted out his punishment. On that day, the breath of Christ will give life and voice to Honour, Honour herself will lament about her loss, about being savagely ravished, about her destruction. Her cries will melt the hearts of the prophets, the silence she had to maintain in this world would be broken by the life-giving breath of Christ himself. Thus awakened, her melodious sorrowful mourning will have the power and the effect to overwhelm all with tears, the loss of Honour's virtue will have the power to move the listener like the sigh of the mother of the martyred Hussain.

We both sat there reflecting, both lost in our own thoughts. I finally broke the silence and turning to Arifa I asked cautiously, 'Should I take some medicine?' Her eyes widened in shock and disbelief and she echoed the word 'medicine?' An involuntary tremor of disgust passed through her body, she looked at me with eyes that seemed to say she found this conversation distasteful.

I think she didn't quite know what to say to me. After I mentioned taking some medicine several times, she lowered her eyes and said quietly, 'Do you have such a medicine?'

It now dawned on me that not only did I not have such a medicine, I also didn't know how to procure something like that. And even if I was somehow able to get it, would I be able to conceal the consequence of taking it?

With great trepidation Arifa advised me that since I really was very unlucky, and that this incident could no longer be kept a secret, and as it really was not my fault, I should abandon the idea of hiding it, and share it with my family. On hearing her suggestion, I trembled with fear and anger. 'Don't be stupid, how can I tell anyone this, and who am I supposed to tell it to? I can't tell the servant girl for even before she tells the family, she would run and announce it to the neighbours and I really can't tell my family myself. Tell me, how am I supposed to address them? How am I supposed to tell them this?'

She had no answers to my questions nor a solution to my problem. All I had been able to achieve was to share it with Arifa. I was now going to go home and suffer the anguish and terror of my obsessive thoughts once again.

9

The Secret Revealed

It had been a week since I visited Arifa. My anxiety and nervousness were increasing day by day. Then I noticed something. A sentence uttered by my mother one day made me realize that she had been aware of what was going on with me, that she had had an inkling all along about what had happened. As soon as I became aware of this, I took a good look at myself. Yes! Yes! There were physical changes in my body that I had been desperately trying to hide. I noticed that my mother had been looking at me closely, suspiciously. At one point I caught her looking at me and when our eyes met we both looked away quickly, as if we were guilty, as if either she or I was a thief.

I was holding the lid of a tin box in my hand when it finally dawned on me that she knew. The lid fell from my hand and hit the ground with a clattering sound. She looked away quickly as if embarrassed for me. I knew then that the secret was out. I ran straight into my room, my heart hammering in my chest. I was soaked in the perspiration of humiliation.

I had not been in my room for more than five minutes when there was some commotion outside my door. I felt as if a knife had been stuck in me. My mouth became dry, I seemed to be losing control over my body. My mother entered the room and approached me slowly. Then she sat on my bed next to me, and placing her hand on my shoulders, she bent over me. It is impossible for anyone to understand the kind of feelings, the emotions, the fear, the humiliation, the pain that I underwent at that moment.

Maintaining a friendly tone, she nudged me, and asked, 'What has happened to you?'

Her questioning me was enough. I lost all restraint and started sobbing uncontrollably. She knew my secret with her mother's heart. She clasped me to her and hugged me tightly and whispered, 'Shhh! Quiet, be quiet!' Then she quickly got up and left the room.

Within half an hour her best friend, who was like her sister, and like an aunt to me, arrived. She and Amma Jaan spoke for a while in low tones. She left my mother and came straight to me and placing her hand on my shoulder, she said, 'Daughter this is not something to hide, nor can you hide it anymore.'

No one can fully understand the state I was in, or know my shame. I was overcome with embarrassment and broke out in a deathly sweat.

Making a long story short, I sobbed and wept and hid my face in my hands, and bit by bit, word by word, I told her my tragic story or rather she got the story out of me. She took a close look at me and then consoled me, offered advice, her love and affection. But at the same time she gently scolded me for keeping this incident secret for so long. How could I tell her that I was silent in the hope that this would all go away by itself?

Finally, she left me and went to my mother and I heard the quiet weeping accompanied by a suppressed scream and I surmised that she had narrated the sordid story to my mother. My mother stopped crying almost immediately out of fear that her state of distress would be witnessed by the very walls, that my story would take wings and spread.

It seemed that suddenly silence descended upon the house and my tragedy was choked to death and put aside. I could hear my mother having a hushed conversation with my father in a closed room. The very next day the whole house seemed to be in a state of doom and gloom. On the surface everything was the same, nothing had changed, and yet everything had changed. It was a tragic silence that seemed to be enveloping the very doors and walls of our house.

I could sense the muted pain and suffering of my family, I could see the looks of patience and forbearance on their sad faces. They were suffering, perhaps even more than if I had died. Yes, the agony and distress that their bodies and souls were going through was greater than that of the death of a loved one. I could see their misery as they went about their daily chores, acting as if nothing had happened. I witnessed their discomfort and dejection. They could find no comfort, whether sitting, standing, sleeping, walking, or talking.

Their hearts were pierced with the slings and arrows of a tragic misfortune. The sharp talons of bitterness and sorrow had gripped their hearts and minds. They wanted to weep and mourn, they wanted to beat their chests and cry out loud, and yet, out of fear of discovery they could not even shed tears.

This was the beginning of my family's collective nightmare. For me, my suffering had just been incrementally doubled. The wrath of God had descended upon me. Indeed it was the wrath of God, to see my beloved and most respected father standing with his head down, his blessed face a picture of extreme melancholy, a sorrow such as I had not seen shroud his whole being, a sorrow greater than he had expressed after the death of my middle brother.

This was a terrifying sorrow, a frightening melancholy that had broken my father's back. The loss of a young, handsome, healthy son had not crushed him as my tragedy had. He was completely defeated. I saw him and my mother standing in the verandah talking in whispers. I saw his face crumble, I saw the struggles within him, as he tried to compose his expression, I saw him lay down his weapons and step out of his armour of manly bravado, the dam burst and rivulets of tears ran down his wrinkled face into his grey beard.

I saw my mother raise her eyes quietly towards her husband. As their eyes met, he pulled his veil of manly demeanour over him, quickly turned his face to the other side and hastily wiped the tears away with his handkerchief. He looked toward the sky, and, suppressing his emotions, he said, 'I'm getting late for court, give me my supper.'

My father's situation was pitiable. In actuality I myself was in a most humiliating and pitiable state. I was the cause of this miserable tragedy. But to see him suffering at his age, I was overcome with compassion for him. *'What must he be thinking?'* Every time I thought of this, I felt close to death.

Amma Jaan very cleverly terminated the services of our maidservant so that there was no one in the house except my father, my mother and myself.

The very house seemed to reverberate with the deafening silence of my tragedy. It seemed that the walls were sighing.

An eerie and frightening silence prevailed. It wasn't just the tragedy but also the dark shadows of destruction that had the entire household in its grip.

This was not like the tragic loss of a young person, time would not heal. This was different, this was going to continue. No one could gauge the extent and continuation of this particular ailment. How does one even try to forget and ignore how society treats criminals like me?

But all this was nothing compared with what was coming. This was just the first few steps towards our destruction. The next stage would be when this secret spread in the neighbourhood, all the way through the narrow street to the market place, becoming cause for titillation and gossip for everyone. And that is what happened. The story of my destruction spread like wildfire, going from the lips of the neighbours to the tops of minarets, of mosques, and the quarters of courtesans.

My public disgrace occurred in a seemingly innocent way. My Khala Bi, my mother's friend to whom I had confessed my entire story, came back the very next day with the most reliable and discreet lady who confirmed what was obvious. This matter can no longer be hidden, she stated matter-of-factly. She had promised secrecy. The very next day Khala Bi was sent to my husband's family to ask for speedy wedding ceremonies.

At the same time another plan had been hatched to hide

my crime. My parents were now planning another crime, to somehow rid me of my present condition and then parcel me off to my husband's home. The lady who had come to examine me refused to take part in this scheme, and now we were surreptitiously looking for some other woman to help me. Somehow during the process of this search my story travelled from my home to the neighbourhood and beyond.

The women from the neighbourhood and others made all kinds of excuses to come and visit us. They could sense the dreadful gloom that permeated in our home. I stayed out of sight, locked in my room, so they didn't see me. They were given excuses for my absence, different stories were handed out to different people. But, as the saying goes, a liar is soon trapped in his lies as his memory fails him.

I couldn't be kept hidden all the time and so some women saw me. There were those who could tell from the sound of a girl's footsteps if she was pregnant or not. One glance was enough to confirm my condition. The neighbourhood knew. Nobody said anything to our face but eventually the gossip spread. Out of concern my father's friends mentioned it to him. 'Why have these people become your enemies? Why are they spreading such rumours about you and your daughter?' they asked.

My parents talked about this and finally realized that there was nothing else to do except to depart for the family home. As soon as we could, we packed up and left, hoping all the while that everybody would think that we had gone to our family home to prepare for my upcoming wedding. And then there was this other matter. What to do about what was ailing me? We did not know how successful Khala Bi had been in convincing my in-laws to move my marriage ceremonies to an earlier date. We were in such a rush to go away that even Bhai Jaan did not know when we left or arrived there.

A few days after we had reached the family home, Khala Bi came with news from my in-laws. They were not ready for the wedding. They were in fact surprised at our eagerness to rush the wedding. We had refused to move the date forward when they had requested it, and now we seemed anxious to move it even earlier than what they had suggested.

Another letter was dispatched to the in-laws in which my parents insisted that they should proceed with the ceremonies as soon as possible since we were at the family home and it would be inconvenient to go back and forth. In the meantime a clever woman who was an expert in her field, was sent for and given the responsibility of taking care of me as soon as possible.

She was given a considerable sum and promised more money later. She said that my condition was advanced and the best time to terminate something like this had been lost. If she was to proceed there would be a danger to my life and she did not want to take responsibility for this. In short, she had taken the money and now she didn't want to finish her work.

God forgive me! Just think about the crime! The Satanic crime! My religious parents, who had given birth to me and raised me so tenderly with such love and affection, had never uttered a harsh word to me, were now willing to sacrifice their principles and my life for the sake of saving their honour. Perhaps this too was my fate. They had raised me to reach an age when an evil man, the devil himself, took advantage of me, and now it seemed that the respect and honour of the family would be lost because I was forcibly ravaged. In order to save this ship named Honour from drowning in this cesspool of filth and degradation, they were ready to sacrifice me. So, the victim that was me was to be victimized twice.

That woman was told categorically that even if I was to die in the process, we were willing to go ahead with it and so now preparations were being made for me to lose my life rather than to lose the family honour and respect. So you see, this was our society, this is how we judged who was honourable and respectable, and who was not. In India it did not matter who committed the crime, it was the victim who was going to pay the price. In this hypocritical society, when the victim of such a crime is punished, the society applauds and declares itself to be honourable, to be respectable, we become proud of ourselves and happy that we are ready to mete out a just punishment to the victim, and we would punish her so harshly that she would wish to be banished to hell with all its fire and brimstone and torture. I myself would have preferred to die and go to hell rather than have to go through all this.

But now not only my mother and father, but I myself was ready to commit another crime to conceal a crime, even if I lost my life in the process.

10

Disaster

Our house was constructed in such a way that anyone who came in first entered through the section called mardana, the men's quarters, after which came a courtyard, and then the second part of the house which was the zenana, the women's quarters. We were lucky that nobody could come into the zenana unnoticed. Any neighbour, friend, family member, anyone coming to the house, had to first walk through the men's section, then through the courtyard, and then enter the women's section. This limited the number of women who could come into the zenana.

So, like a modest bride-to-be, if I knew that somebody was coming in, I would go into my own darkened room and lock myself in. Amma Jaan had instructed me that regardless of however much she, or someone else insisted that I come out, I was not to do so.

So we played this charade. Family members, neighbours, and friends would come, Amma Jaan would stand outside in the verandah and scold me, insisting that I come out, but I would plead shyness and not show myself. A few aggressive women did manage to push their way into my room. I would not bother to get up. I would say my salaam to them and turn my face away. Discouraged by my general attitude, they would go away disappointed, but full of suspicion. Meanwhile my treatment for my ailment had started in full force.

After one week of being treated with various potions, I became exceedingly ill, and for a while it seemed like both of us would not be able to make it. As a matter of fact, there was the fear that both of us would die within a matter of hours. The lady who was treating me became very alarmed, stopped her treatment, and tried instead to save my life. In the meantime, while my medical treatment was in progress, my in-laws were being persuaded to expedite the wedding.

All of this coming and going of letters and messengers resulted in my in-laws setting a date for the final wedding day. Also, after a few days of treatment I became well again, and my treatment to rid me of the unwelcome visitor resumed. It seemed as if the treatment was working, but just when it seemed like all my troubles were going to be over soon and a successful marital life was within my grasp, a new calamity arose and this was a monstrous disaster.

It was not our enemies who inflicted this near fatal attack on us, rather these were the enemies of the lady who was treating me. They had no interest in harming us, but they certainly wanted to punish her for whatever it was they held against her. She was reported for criminal activities to the police. The police arrested this woman. She had been arrested twice before for a similar crime and had suffered dire consequences. The police used physical abuse to obtain a confession regarding her nefarious activities, which she provided and within a matter of days my father was requested to report at the police station.

My innocent father had no idea what was in store for him. He thought perhaps his opinion was needed for something that had happened in the neighbourhood and he arrived there completely unprepared, completely confident. But on his return from the police station he appeared to be half the man he was. He entered the house and fell into a faint on the floor.

Amma Jaan and all of us thought that this had to do with exhaustion. But very soon we discovered the real reason for his condition. I broke out in a cold sweat and was about to faint as well. The crux of the matter was that a lawsuit was in progress, and not just my honour, but the family's honour and respect were now on the line. It was just a matter of days before this news would be all over town.

Very soon I was able to find out the details of what had transpired and realized how delicate this matter was and how complicated. You can imagine what we were going through, we had no other choice but to sacrifice whatever money, assets, jewellery, and property that had been prepared for my wedding, and give it over for this lawsuit. At the same time, we would have to bribe the police so that this matter could be quietly resolved. There's an old saying that problems don't come singly, and now I knew that it wasn't just our respect and our good name that we were going to lose, but we were also going to face penury.

It would be hard to describe the agony and state of terror we were in for those days. I wouldn't wish on my worst enemy what I was going through. Perhaps this was all part of my fate. Obviously my treatment had come to a standstill as we were now running back and forth to police stations and to lawyers.

One of the clerks at the police station, who carried quite a lot of weight, developed a great deal of sympathy for my father's plight after he heard the sordid details of my violation. He decided to help us and that too without accepting a single penny, although there was one condition that he imposed; no further treatment was to be sought by my family to terminate what God had given me. If we reneged on this condition the lawsuits would restart with a vengeance. My father tried to dissuade him from imposing this condition, but he was adamant.

We were now back to square one. We were under time constraints as on my father's insistence, my in-laws had decided to oblige him by expediting the marriage date. This new date was fast approaching, each day brought us closer and closer to a final, disastrous revelation. The marriage date appeared to be a lot more frightening than the date of my death.

My father didn't sleep for three full nights and on the third night he gave up. He accepted final defeat. He did what men do when they feel completely lost and vanquished. Tired, exhausted, panic-stricken that somehow my in-laws would find out, each day brought him closer and closer to a state of complete desperation, defeat and madness. Losing all hope, he did what desperate people do when they are cornered.

At around 2 a.m. in the morning I heard my mother's screams. I ran in my bare feet to her room. She was sitting on the bed, wringing her hands and pulling her hair. My father had attempted suicide. He had ingested poison. We did not have any servants anymore, they had all been let go so that nobody could find out what was going on in our home. There was just a young houseboy who was rudely awakened and sent at once to get one of the men in the neighbourhood who in turn was asked to go to my father's brother with the news. As suicide was against the law, a doctor couldn't be summoned to take care of my father since he would have to inform the authorities. My uncle found a hakim, a homeopath who was a friend of his who came and after an examination determined that my father had tried to kill himself by swallowing opium. My mother confirmed it. She knew this because he had discussed this with her that very evening. She had cried and begged and made him promise that he would not undertake such a sinful solution. He had placated her with a false promise.

Hakim Sahib came up with a solution. My father was given tincture of ipecac which made him vomit several times. For once luck was with us and he was revived after several episodes of vomiting. For two days and two nights his condition was extremely delicate, his pulse was fast, his breathing shallow, and he lay in bed in a coma as if dead. We could barely wake him up. But on the third day he seemed to be somewhat recovered. Hakim sahib reassured us that by the grace of God he was out of danger.

I don't want to repeat what we were going through; it seems as though I'm continuously telling the same story again and again. Oh my God! What was to happen next? Here was my father in his weakened condition and here was I, in the same condition as before. And the date of my marriage was fast approaching. The fifth day after the suicide attempt, it was decided after a great deal of discussion that the best solution was to once again approach my in-laws and this time try to persuade them to agree to a later date. With that another letter was composed and once again a courier was dispatched to persuade my in-laws to change the date yet once again, the reasoning being that my father was not well. The very next day we received a wire from my in-laws, stating very clearly that they had made all the preparations, that they had informed all the relatives, that everybody had gathered for this auspicious occasion. They wished my father speedy recovery and prayed for his good health and said they were unable to change the date of the wedding. They hoped that my father would recover completely and only if his condition deteriorated further, would they be willing to consider changing the date. They also stated that if we changed the date once more then the wedding would take place after a longer period of time, as it would be very difficult for them to make these preparations again, and to get the entire family together again. All I can say is that their line of thought was completely reasonable.

Once again, there was a lot of confusion and discussion in the family. Another wire was sent to them and once again the request was made to advance the date. A very quick reply came back from them once again, saying they were praying for my father's speedy recovery and that they could not change the date. However, if something inauspicious happened they would have to cancel the wedding. And now once more it was decided by the family that there was really nothing else to do except to start treating me to terminate my situation, even though my father had promised that he would not take part in such measures this time.

I wished that the sky would part or that the earth beneath my feet with split open and swallow me, that a snake would sting me and speedily deliver me to my final destination. A girl whose father, uncles, mother and the rest of the family were suffering because of her undesirable condition, deserved to die. I wouldn't wish this situation on my worst enemy, I really do believe that nobody could understand my situation, no one could really imagine how deplorable all this was and how all of it had corrupted and made criminals of us all. My pious father who had performed his tahajudh, the pre-dawn prayer, since his youth, a man known for his uprightness, honesty and integrity, was today helpless in the face of our impending doom, for what is a man without honour? And the women of the family are flag bearers of this honour, we who are raised all our life with the motto, 'Lose your life before your honour'. And the maintenance of this honour required all kinds of deceit, lies, intrigues—such despicable acts. May God protect me! Whereas once a mere splinter under my skin aroused such pain and tenderness in my parent's bosom, now my very life was being put in danger to avoid disgrace.

Since Hakim Sahib was a great friend of my uncle, there was not much that was kept secret from him. It was now decided that this whole sordid affair was going to be revealed to him, he was going to be asked to help us. If you think about it, why would anybody participate in an activity that the police already knew about, that had been dismissed only recently at great emotional and psychological expense? When Hakim sahib was asked about helping us, he became quite distressed and said very clearly that he had never ever treated anyone for something like this before, adding that he had no experience in terminating such a condition. He could not do it himself nor would he give advice as to how we could do it. My uncle and my father put a great deal of pressure on Hakim Sahib. He was told he was responsible for our honour, our respect. Finally, very reluctantly, and with great trepidation he agreed to listen to all the details about how twice termination had been attempted and had failed. He inquired after the lady who had treated me, he questioned her about the medications she had given me, and after spending quite a bit of time going over the entire history of the case, he told us in clear terms that the only way it could be done could cost me my life. Even if I somehow survived, I may be left with certain physical and mental defects that might be unacceptable for most people. Also, after such a treatment I may not be able to get up from my bed for six to seven months.

After hearing all this I became extremely frightened. I looked at my elders who had decided that I should be treated regardless of how dangerous it was for my health and for my life since the date of my marriage was arriving soon and they could not deal with the scandals that would follow. While everybody else had no consideration about what was going to happen to me, I was full of doubt. I realized that I did not want to die. I did not want to be left as a damaged, defective person. I knew what the previous treatment had been like, I knew how close to death I had come and it was clear to me that no one was concerned about my life or health. This time Hakim Sahib had made it clear that I would once again be faced with the danger of death and serious and quite likely permanent side-effects. I thought about it for a long time and I thought, even if I died, this story was not going to remain within these four walls, this story of my disgrace was certain to go out, this story was going to make it to the town square, everyone was going to find out sooner or later. It didn't matter whether I was treated or not, it didn't matter if the treatment worked or not, it didn't matter if I died or not, my family and I were doomed to be dishonoured. I don't know how, but I turned into a completely shameless and bold woman and very quietly and firmly I told my mother that I would not undergo this treatment.

I no longer felt shy, embarrassed, or timid. Somehow this entire experience, along with my father's illness, when my mother and I were the only ones taking care of him, had emboldened me. My father and my uncle and others of my family were quite shocked at my decision. In fact, not only were they shocked, they were quite angry with me and becoming extremely agitated, they tried to persuade me to reconsider. I on the other hand decided that I was not going to undergo any more treatments. I was not prepared to go through any of it again. The entire family disapproved of and disagreed with this decision. They didn't think it was a decision that I should be allowed to make. However, Hakim Sahib was now on my side. It is possible that he was relieved since he had not wanted to take part in this treatment in the first place. He reminded them, repeatedly, that treating me for this would be the same as taking my life.

My mother became furious with me. She turned to me in anger and shouted, 'You shameless, unlucky girl! Your life is so important to you that you don't care about your father's and your grandfather's honour? Tell me, what do you plan to do now? Tell me how we are to take care of this problem?'

I remained silent at first but finally gave her an answer. In the calmest and most respectful way possible, I pleaded with her. 'Please, please get me to my husband's home somehow. I will deal with whatever happens there to me, I will convince him that it was not my fault.'

I was no longer afraid, my pathetic and unavoidable

situation was forcing me to take refuge behind my innocence. As a matter of fact, in talking about my innocence, I gained a new sense of strength; I felt renewed and rejuvenated once I was able to voice my innocence; I felt that all that had happened so far was because of my weakness. I should not have been frightened in the first place. I should not be frightened or intimidated by people who would call me names. Actually I would dare anybody to say anything to my face, there was no need for me to hide like a thief or a criminal. I knew I was innocent, truly innocent, even if my husband didn't believe me, I was ready to look into his eyes and state as boldly as possible that I was not the sinner, rather, a crime had been committed against me.

This change in my attitude, this shift from cowering and self-blame to confidence and resolve, surprised me. Why had I been I hiding my face from the world until now? Why was I willing to allow myself to be labelled a cheat, a sinner, a criminal? I found myself talking very firmly and harshly with my mother, clearly telling her that there was no need for me to be treated in this manner.

'You just send me to my husband's home, I will deal with what happens there, I will deal with my life.'

Hakim Sahib was my biggest supporter. He nodded and said, 'A husband is a husband. And if the girl feels so strongly about it, and she is truly innocent as we know, then God will help and God will put compassion in a husband's heart.'

This went on for a few days. All kinds of pressure was being thrust upon me, but I remained firm in my determination: I would not undergo any further treatment. Finally, they all decided to leave me to my fate. I realized that I had to use my strength, my innocence, to treat my defeated family and to renew their energy and life once again. The details of my disaster were locked in the bosoms of some extremely dependable and trustworthy individuals. I felt confident that I would be able to reach my husband's home, and after that, it was going to be up to me to deal with it.

Witnessing my resolve, my mother very quickly made me sit in my room for the mayun ceremony in which the bride is secluded for a few days before the wedding. Now that I was a bride-to-be in the literal sense of the word, planning began in earnest for my wedding. My mother became so absorbed in the preparations that I think she forgot what else had been going on.

My own feelings at this point did not have the highs and the lows that I had experienced before. Instead, I was filled with determination and confidence, although at least twice a day I would lose all confidence and feel as if I was falling apart. I trembled as if I could see disaster staring at me with a ghoulish look in its eyes. That was when I would then grab the spears of my confidence and pierce those eyes.

With each passing day I could feel my strength and

confidence waning. But I was not in pain, it was as if I had become used to my problems. It was rather like a chronic illness, like a cancer. The acute pain of the original discovery was no longer there, but the constant discomfort, fear and restlessness of the malignant condition I was in, remained. I was waiting for my wedding like one waits for one's death. I could see the steamroller of time rolling towards me with all its weight and it was going to crush me.

There were very few days left and time passed rather quickly. There was a stillness like the quiet before a storm. On the surface it seemed everything was peaceful and safe, but as the day of the wedding approached, I could sense and smell the oncoming apocalypse. I was going to be swept away in that coming storm, I was going to be swept away in that deadly whirlpool that would suck in my family's honour and respect and they would be caught in that vortex, like a ship that was wrecked and would soon sink. Everyone knew deep in their hearts that there was no way I would accompany my husband to my new home without a disturbance that would reveal all. Every one of my family members knew that before any good could come out of this oncoming marriage, there was going to be a storm. It was more than possible that we would all be swept away in it. Actually, this is what disaster really is.

11

Cataclysmic Disaster

I will never forget that moment when the house was full of guests. I saw my wedding finery lying on my bed. Finally, my confidence, my strength began to waver. With the passage of time my resolution had weakened. As I was putting on my wedding attire I began to feel overwhelmed. I did not deserve to wear this outfit; I was insulting this very outfit; I was deceiving everyone; I was a cunning, lying, treacherous, pretender, a fraud, I was devious and sly. This outfit which represented purity and innocence did not belong on my person, it was meant for a virtuous bride or could be the outfit of a widow, but a woman like me who was using her veil to hide her deceit, her double-dealing, had no right to don this outfit. All of this pomp and show, it was soon going to be turned into a tragic drama, the deception would be detected and blow the cover of this outfit like dynamite.

The barat, the wedding party, arrived ceremoniously, the groom with his sehra, the flower garlands, the band, the female singers singing wedding songs, my mother-in-law in her grand outfit, the jewellery of the women, the airs they put on. Their accommodations were close by, they had made lavish arrangements and appeared to be in a joyous, celebratory mood. Meanwhile, dressed in all my finery, my mental state in turmoil, I was trying to keep a grip on my emotions, but when I heard that now the wedding party had arrived to conduct the final traditional rituals of the marriage ceremony, I once again started to tremble. *'Look at us!'* I thought bitterly. *'Look at our brashness, our impudence, our unmitigated gall and audacity. And what is going to be the result of all of this when I finally reach my husband's home? This whole matter will be exposed. What will happen then? Perhaps they would be too embarrassed and in order to save their own honour and respect they will accept me. Even if we believe this unbelievable scenario, what then? What happens next? This is not just a matter of a day, this is a matter of a lifetime. Unh! I will deal with it when the time comes.'*

Despite what was happening, whatever I was feeling, these emotions, these thoughts that were running obsessively through my mind, the guests were busy with the celebrations and had no knowledge of it. I suppose my family was also going through their own doubts, but they had not a moment to spare since they were occupied with entertaining the guests, going through the festivities. I realized that this was not a wedding, but a high-scale, elaborately orchestrated heist.

The wedding guests entered our home with great ceremony. My husband's family was received with all the Eastern hospitality we are known for. I was completely exhausted by then. I sat on my bed only half awake, feeling as if my soul had left my body. My mother had made such strict arrangements that nobody could come close to me. The only people who were allowed near me were those who were aware of my predicament. I could no longer hold back. I was slowly falling apart, unravelling. My weeping, my crying, my swoons, these were all mistaken as part of my modest and shy demeanour, for an Eastern bride is supposed to be reluctant, sad and faint at the time of her wedding. My condition was attributed to this expected and normal behaviour, and much admired by all, for this is what a bride leaving her parents' home is supposed to demonstrate as proof of her love for her parents.

The women of my husband's family approached me to carry out all sorts of traditional ceremonies, a process imbued with the danger of discovery. It had to be managed with care and delicacy by close family members who surrounded me.

My in-laws were made to believe that they were looking at me and yet it had to be done in such a way that they did not see the full picture. It was the most skillfully orchestrated operation. One false step and all would be lost. This feat had to be accomplished with great cleverness and cunning and a special sleight-of-hand.

A sudden general hush followed almost immediately by loud exclamations, laughter and excitement was enough to inform me that the groom was on his way. It was as if an earthquake had occurred in the house. Everyone was filled with excitement because a groom is such a spectacle. I heard it whispered that the groom had come in a motorcar rather than on a mount as was the custom.

All the guests were chattering loudly about his manly appearance. I heard a detailed description of the handsome groom. Girls jumped and shouted all around him. Young maidens tittered and screamed in delight. Old ladies strained their voices in making loud comments about the groom's good looks. All of these messages were reaching my ears.

Some talked about his height and his build, others talked about his abundant hair and his dreamy eyes, some commented on his beguiling smile. How dapper! How smart! How well-groomed! How debonair! How elegant! Dashing and chic. There were others who compared him to other grooms they had recently witnessed at some other weddings and those poor men were torn and ripped into pieces. All this which should have been music to my ears, all of this that would have made a bride's heart fill with joy, that would have made a newly married young girl feel proud and grateful for her good luck, all of this made me feel so inconsequential, so small, so undeserving and such a cheat.

It seemed that the worst was over. Actual ceremonies were about to start when a rumour flew in on a butterfly's wings that the groom had gone to visit his friend for a couple of minutes, and that too, at his friend's request. This was soon followed by a louder whisper that the groom had been gone a long time. His presence was greatly awaited. My mother-in-law and a few other ladies from my husband's family came and performed some perfunctory ceremonies and then left. The whispers that the groom had disappeared began to grow louder and louder.

The groom's family was also getting concerned, the elders of his family annoyed with his behaviour. His father was no longer living, his uncles, both his maternal and paternal uncles, were now the elders of the family. The news was arriving by the minute into the lady's arena that these elders were getting very angry at the groom for leaving so suddenly, without any explanation. This was how the groom's family was behaving so just think what we were going through.

As soon as I heard this news, I turned cold with anxiety, then I heard a woman say that the police inspector of this area was a friend of the groom. Don't forget that my husband was also training to become a police officer. Remember also the accusation that was launched against my father that was confirmed in the near past. My heart started to beat violently. Are the police going to expose me?

The thought made me feel I was dying once again. My mother and the others who were involved in our conspiracy also became agitated, and very soon we found out that his friend had unceremoniously informed the groom about my plight. Apparently the police inspector was of a double mind; on the one hand he felt sorry for us, for what we had undergone, and on the other he wanted to exercise his loyalty toward his friend. He had asked the groom to join him and taking him to the police station had showed him all of the written evidence, and said to him, 'Everything is in front of you, do what you think is best.'

The groom was also a police officer so he asked for the woman who was treating me to come forward, and then questioned her. While this was still going on his uncle arrived at the station, fuming and frothing at the mouth. To calm down his uncle the groom pointed to the midwife who was involved in the fiasco and placed all the evidence in front of him. Now both of them had disappeared.

Meanwhile, where a short while ago wedding celebrations were in progress, now all kinds of gossip and innuendo echoed in the house. Another group was sent to find the groom and the uncle and they too did not return. It was just a matter of time before all the women were also whispering and wondering what was going on. Our house had changed from a place of joyous celebration to a house filled with mourning. The sky had fallen upon us.

I felt my life draining from my body, my heart skipped several beats, and then it felt as if it had stopped. I felt my hands, my arms and my legs tingling with fear. My mouth turned dry and darkness flooded over me; the room began to swim before my eyes, and I held onto the bed I was sitting on. After that I don't know what happened, I think I fainted.

While I was lying in a deep faint the groom's family was planning their retreat. First they all formed a group, and after a lengthy muffled discussion, an older woman from their side came over to talk to my mother. She said to my mother, 'Sister what is the matter? There is something that does not seem right here, tell me what is the matter? I need to see the bride myself, I need to examine the bride.'

My mother became so distraught that instead of coming up with some kind of excuse she said that there was no way that the bride could be shown to her or to anybody. When the lady asked why, she was told the bride had fainted because she was leaving her parents' home. At this the lady said, 'I can still examine her.' At which point my mother came up with a bright idea and said, 'Well, once she has gone to your home you can take a good look at her.'

You can well imagine what the result would be of such a strange and awkward conversation. The elderly lady kept insisting, my mother kept refusing. It didn't take a special intellect to understand what was going on.

Then this news was taken outside, among the men. With a great deal of cunning and pretence, my family claimed total innocence and surprise. There was a general confusion among the groom's family. They didn't know how to behave, no one had ever encountered such a situation. Some thought they should leave right away. Others were of the opinion that leaving so suddenly would be an insult to the groom, although some of them believed that the groom had already been insulted and the situation was out of control. There were those who proclaimed loudly that the groom had refused to accept me. To be very honest, nobody likes to drink a glass of milk with a fly in it. Deep down in my heart I did not blame him. Anyone in this situation would have done the same.

The nikah papers, involving a mehr of 20,000 rupees, and already signed and notarized, made the nikah valid. If the groom and his family wanted to divorce me, they would have to pay this mehr. This was a point that gave the groom's family pause. They realized that they could not make this decision in haste. They were huddled together, trying to come up with the next option.

The solution they arrived at was that they were not

going to take me with them as the bride. However, they promised that as a family they would think about the next step. Essentially the decision was not to take me with them. A few hours ago the wedding party had arrived with great fanfare, accompanied with a band, horse-drawn colourful buggies, dancing girls and the groom's flower-laden car, and now they crept away in silence.

It's a good thing that I did not see them leave. I was in a swoon for over two hours. Then Hakim Sahib was sent for, smelling salts were brought out, medicines were administered. I finally woke up, although whenever I tried to raise my head from the pillow, I became dizzy and started to retch. Even though there were a lot of guests in the house, I could sense that the air in our house was one of deep mourning. It was as if I had died. There I was, in the bridal chamber, attired in my wedding finery. I felt as if I was wrapped in a shroud, waiting to be buried. It seemed as if the guests were there not to attend a wedding but to participate in a funeral prayer. My eyes were open, but I could neither move nor talk. This final act of public humiliation, of my tragedy, had completely broken my spirit. A flood of tears was pouring out like a river and I couldn't stop it. My very blood had turned into the tears that were pouring out of my eyes. As I lay there silently, I was informed that they had all left. I had been so crushed by the weight of my assault, the burden of my secrets, the heaviness of my sadness, and now my very spirit was being crushed, I felt as if the stone lid of a ten-ton sarcophagus lay on my breast, I felt my soul was ready to leave my body. Even in that state the thought that my poor father and my uncle had to undergo this public humiliation and shame was what was killing me, making me weep more. I felt as if my heartbeat was slowing down, my heart was rising to my throat and choking me. I sobbed silently. I would have these fits of weeping that would just keep increasing in intensity until I was completely spent, my body would start shaking uncontrollably and I would turn cold as ice. I began hiccupping with exhaustion, I was unable to breathe. My whole body would convulse and shudder and I would go into a state in which I was neither living or dead. In that state of limbo, I would feel alive for a few moments and then the cycle would repeat itself. My face was buried in my pillow which, along with my handkerchief, was soaking wet.

The whole household was grieving. Everyone had accepted defeat, except my uncle who loved me like his own and believed in my innocence. He got up determinedly and without any shame or hesitation, arrived at the groom's residence. He boldly demanded that he be allowed to talk to the groom alone. My in-laws stood firm. They insisted that he could talk to the groom, but not alone. 'You have to do it in front of us.'

My uncle did talk to the family. I'm not sure what he said

or what they said. He came back exhausted, disappointed, and empty-handed. However, he did seem somewhat gratified by the fact that the groom's family was equally saddened on finding out what had happened. My husband's family swore that they would seek out the enemy, that they would share our state of dishonour and loss of respect.

When Amma Jaan heard all this, she became very agitated and started crying loudly while praying in favour of her son-in-law, my husband the groom, saying he should find it in his heart to accept me. Then she began cursing the man who had abused me, and sitting on the prayer mat, she rocked, wept, prayed and cursed.

'God in heaven,' she cried. 'This torture! This disaster! This tragedy! This cruelty that has been inflicted upon me should be inflicted upon the assailant and his family. The way he has disgraced and dishonoured us, he too should suffer such disgrace, lightning should strike him.'

Her curses bore the heartache of a distressed mother. On hearing my mother go on so, I too realized that I should join her in cursing my assailant. I prayed that the fate that had befallen me, should also befall my assailant's wife. I cursed and prayed that his wife should also be sexually assaulted and abused, that the way I had been disrespected and exposed, she too should suffer suspicion and exposure.

I kept thinking about that infamous day, furious at myself. When he was leaving, the knife was lying there, why didn't I grab that knife and plunge it into his back, I was strong enough to have killed him despite my physical frailty. I should have at least tried, I should have, I should have. Filled with regret I somehow wanted to go back to that moment and plunge that knife in his back.

The day came to an end and all the guests left, one by one, and finally our house became dark and empty. Conversations about what had happened and what was to be done next continued, while there were also discussions with the in-laws. Finally, the groom's family stated openly that they were going to leave the next day and they did not want anything to do with us. As far as they were concerned, the disgrace was all ours and had nothing to do with them.

This was the most frightening dark night of my entire life and I will never forget it. I kept shifting through episodes of weeping and then calming down, only to once again have the sorrow overcome me and I would once again find myself sobbing hysterically. Exhausted by my own emotions I fell asleep after midnight and I had an extremely frightening nightmare.

PART THREE

12

Vampire

I saw that our whole house was ablaze with a soft gold light and suffused with the fragrance of fresh spring flowers, and the sweet warm breaths of the angels of love. My bridal chamber smelled pure and sweet, I heard some sounds, pleasant, celebratory and soothing in nature. I was dressed in my bridal finery. I was waiting eagerly, anxiously for someone.

I could hear guests talking, I could smell their perfumes, I could hear the tinkling of their bangles and anklets, the sensual silky rustle of their attire whispered in my ears, I was sitting with my head bent, a gossamer veil covered my face and of all the sounds, the loudest sound I could hear was the beating of my heart.

Suddenly I heard whispers at my door that were pleasing to my ear. The door swung open on its hinges with a soft sound. I felt a cool breeze, heady with the fragrance of fresh flowers. I realized, no, I knew who it was! My heart was filled with a strange sensation. I was anxious and excited, pleased and nervous. I felt a hand on my left shoulder and then I was pulled up gently. I almost tripped on my wedding dress, got up and started walking in the direction where I was being led. I was walking with my husband. I was leaving with him. I heard the sounds of the shehnai playing the song of the bride's departure.

I had barely stepped out of my room when suddenly my husband grabbed both my shoulders and shook me and pushed me away. In a voice shaking with anger he said, 'This is deception!' Before I could utter a word, he had left me. I saw his back, he was wearing the wedding achkan, the same Banarasi achkan, that had been sent to him by my family to wear on the wedding day. I saw those golden embroidered flowers on the back of his achkan, they seemed to be winking at me, twinkling with a blinding glare.

On seeing him leave like that, I became agitated and ran after him. He was ahead of me and I was chasing him. I was running very fast behind him at this point. I didn't know where I was. And I didn't know where he was going. But I was pursuing him. We were now running, he in front and I behind him, in a very large square that was completely deserted, dismal and dark. There was no other person in that square. There was a grey mist that surrounded us. No! No! Perhaps it was smoke, and then perhaps, it was just the veil of the deep sadness of the entire world.

All around us was this deep, eerie silence. A terrifying silence. I was frightened and stumbling, and yet I kept running after him as if possessed. It suddenly seemed as if I was gaining on him. I was getting nearer and nearer, I could see the Banarasi silk achkan with the bright gold flowers right in front of me, so close that I could touch them. He stopped and then he turned around to look at me.

I saw his face. May God have mercy! A muffled scream escaped from my throat, fear and terror paralyzed me, I couldn't move. It was not my husband, it was a monster, it was a vampire. Completely horrified and yet as though hypnotized, I couldn't move. My blood froze in my veins.

I just stood there, looking at him. The skin on his face was black and scaly, covered with oozing, pustular boils, his eyes were yellow like those of a feral animal, his mouth was vile, with a smug smile on his fleshy thick lips which were of a deep purple colour. His large, sharp, yellowing teeth were stained with blood. His expression was completely satanic.

I had never seen such a frightening face in my entire life, a face that was so ugly, so petrifying, that one felt instant revulsion and hatred. I pray no one ever sees a face like that. He smiled and I saw his red bleeding gums, his sharp yellow teeth. I stumbled back a few steps. His thick lips moved as if to say something, but what came out of his mouth was like the snarl of a predator, the hissing of a snake. He extended his filthy hand towards me. No! It was not a hand, it was a claw with long, dirt-encrusted nails that looked like the claws of a vulture. I shrank back.

That creature moved his head away from me, he started walking again, I just kept staring at his back. After walking a few steps, he turned his head and looked at me again. The shock of what I saw made me scream once again. It was not the vampire. It was my assailant, the man who had sexually assaulted me. Before I could regain my senses, he turned and started walking away. After a few steps he turned again and it was that creature. He took some steps, turned, and I saw that it was the face of my assailant.

This happened repeatedly. The two forms alternated each time this two-faced monster turned around. He walked faster and faster, he got further and further away from me, and yet I could see his two faces in all their detail. He was moving away from me rapidly, the two faces were rotating and alternating with greater speed. These mechanized rotating faces were moving so rapidly that I started getting dizzy. Even though he was moving away from me, I could see everything. After a while he disappeared.

But I kept seeing the two forms even though they were not there. Their presence had become a black dot far, far away on the horizon. For a while it seemed as though all motion had ceased, I felt as if this black dot was staring at me. Its appearance changed into a black star, its intensity was overwhelming, the black colour turned deeper and darker. I couldn't take my eyes off it. It started moving towards me.

Then it began to increase in size, it started to rise in the sky. It floated up in the sky. It rose up and up like a full moon except it was black. There was a dark halo around it. It emanated black rays that raced towards the earth with lightning speed. Darkness seemed to be descending on the earth, this darkness that was fast enveloping the world, was ice cold and was accompanied by a satanic silence.

There was a sudden explosion so loud that I cringed and ducked my head, covering my ears with my hands. The explosion was accompanied by a fast-moving piece of that black moon shaped like a cannon ball billowing smoke behind it. It flew over my head and kept going, leaving a black streak behind it. As I tried to see where it was going to fall, following it with my eyes, I heard a loud tortured cry from somewhere not too far. It was a tortured woman's agonizing scream. Ahhh! Ahhh! Ahhh!

I heard that bloodcurdling scream and without any regard to personal safety I ran towards it, though I could see nothing. The descending darkness cast eerie shadows that were most deceptive. The screams seemed to be echoing everywhere, it was hard to determine where they were coming from. Finally I saw some shadows in the distance, I ran towards them and saw a young beautiful girl whose eyes were shut, whose face was pale as if she was bloodless and her facial expression was that of someone in pain. She was in the arms of the monster, the vampire I had seen earlier.

He bared his teeth and dug them into her delicate neck. Blood was dripping down his chin, the very skin of her lovely neck was ripped apart, he was sucking her lifeblood. As he sucked her blood, wolf-like guttural growls emanated from his throat. I noticed that there was another face on the other side of this monster's face. That was the face of my assailant. He looked at me with deep anger and hatred. I realized that these two creatures were in reality one.

I couldn't take it anymore and let out a cry, 'Dear God! Is there no justice in your world? Is there no one who will save the innocent?' These words had barely left my mouth when I saw lightning ripping across the sky. The light seemed to be directed at a figure that was slowly descending from the dark sky and as it got closer, I saw it was him, wearing the same Banarsi achkan, his face covered with a sehra of flowers. He held a bow and arrow in his hands. He shot the arrow towards that black star, the arrow whizzed up! Up! It pierced the black star which shattered with a loud sound into a thousand pieces. The shards from the black star chimed and then dissipated with a small moan. A bright light appeared and started to grow, gradually slicing the darkness as it faded away.

Suddenly the world was filled with a pure, blessed light. I saw something alight near me. I ran towards it. There was a curtain behind which was the same man who had shot the arrow. I lifted up the curtain and tried to take a good look at this man. It all seemed hazy and I couldn't see very well. As I got closer, I saw my own face, I saw myself looking beautiful and happy. There was a loud noise and suddenly everything disappeared; the magic was gone, the square was gone, the man with the bow and arrow was gone. I was in my room, I was standing in front of the mirror, looking at my own image.

A large porcelain vase which was close to the mirror had fallen and shattered into a thousand pieces, that was the noise that I had heard. I saw my own face in the mirror, smiling and looking happy. But then! Then my reality suddenly dawned on me; a noise between a sob and a scream escaped from my throat, and I held my spinning head in both my hands as I realized that nothing had changed.

It was morning, things were still the same, I was the same, the house was still in mourning. Everyone was still talking about the barat that had left me behind, that had refused to take me with them, that was going to leave for good today. The pain and the anger, the frustration and the tears, seemed to rise once more within my chest. I tried to hang on to this nightmare, this impossible dream, I tried to interpret it as something in my favour, I tried to console myself, but naked reality was in front of me.

The fact that I had now been completely exposed, and publicly humiliated and disgraced, could not be denied; nobody was going to forgive me. But I had thought in my dreams that I had heard the words 'Your problems will be solved.' Maybe I imagined that. Amma Jaan was insisting that we should go to the groom's family and try to convince them that my disgrace and my dishonour, was in reality their disgrace and their dishonour, that they should stand by me to save their own self-respect. I was convinced that my dream was going to be fulfilled.

13

Wrong Interpretation

My uncle went to the groom's family once again, he once again argued and pleaded and gave them my mother's message. They gave a very clear answer. They said, 'We've made up our minds, we are not taking the bride with us. Please don't try to convince us about something we are not willing to agree to. Nor are we willing to discuss it any further.' They would not let him talk to the groom, and in fact refused to even allow him to meet him.

My family had taken the position that as I was married into their family, I really was a member of their family, that this injustice and cruelty had been suffered by a member of their family. The shame and humiliation was all theirs, not ours.

'This whole tragic incident had absolutely nothing to do with our family. This insult is now yours and you do what you want.'

I had now been officially abandoned by my own family. I was no longer one of them.

The groom's family accepted that, yes, I now was a married member of their family, but they couldn't accept me because I was of no use to them. The groom himself did not want to have anything to do with the bride.

A few other respected elders also approached them, but their arguments and pleading were of no avail. The answer was that I was not going to be accepted by them. I had been convinced after my dream/nightmare last night that my life would be sorted out for once and for all. What a foolish interpretation, I thought bitterly.

It was around two o'clock in the afternoon when the family realized that all their efforts had finally failed. There was nothing they could do about this. The only thing we could do, as a family, was to weep and cry about our misfortune. I too was in that state, but I pulled myself together. I was no longer afraid. I had lost everything, there was nothing more to lose. After some more outbursts of weeping and feeling sorry for myself, I realized it would have been better if I had met my husband at least once, so that I could explain why I was innocent. I was sure that my family members had explained it all to him, but I would have liked to have told him myself about what had happened. Not just because he should take me with him, but that he should believe that I was a victim, that I was innocent. I convinced myself that as I was not responsible for what had happened, I should be able to talk to him. I wanted to appeal to his humanity. I thought about convincing him that I should, not now, but later on, in a few days perhaps, come back with him. He could keep me in his home like a servant girl. Because in all honesty that was the best status I could now aspire to.

These kinds of plots kept running through my mind. Finally, I went to my mother, who was crying. I explained very clearly to her that I wished I had met my husband, that I wished I had been able to tell him my story. She listened very carefully to what I had to say and after thinking about it for a little while she asked me how I thought I would achieve this plan.

'There is no purpose, no plan,' I said. 'But I am his legal wife. I will tell them that I'm in trouble and that as my husband he has a duty towards me, and even if he doesn't want to take me with him, he should help me.'

I made it very clear to her that it was my life that was on the line, everybody had tried and failed, now I was going to try my own luck. I turned around and started to leave.

Amma Jaan was surprised and becoming agitated. She asked, 'Are you going to go by yourself?'

I turned back towards her and answered, 'No, I will ask him to come to me.'

She frowned and asked, 'What if he doesn't come?'

I shook my head. I went back to my room and quickly wrote a letter. *'You have faced a lot of dishonour and disrespect and there is more to come. I'm not sure what you have heard. But the truth? Do you know the truth? Absolutely not. Then why are you trying to slaughter me with a dull knife. If you have any self-respect then please remember I'm your lawfully wedded wife. It is my duty also to make you fully aware of the incident, this is something that perhaps a woman cannot tell anyone except her husband. But tell me, how am I to explain the reality to you? Before you take any action, please don't make a hasty decision based on what you have heard; please try to find out the truth, after you have found out the truth you may do as you please. At least meet me for a couple of minutes. If you decide not to grant me my request and want to make a decision based on gossip, you are entitled to do so, I will complain not to you but to my destiny. I once again repeat that you have suffered disrespect and there is more to come. I would like for you to spare me two minutes of your time to find out the truth, the reality. The decision is up to you.*

Yours, the unfortunate one.'

My mother called the old barber who was a trusted servant. He was to be the messenger. My mother said, 'Khalifa Ji if you can do this work for me, and it results in the completion of my heart's, desire I will give you gold bracelets.' After thus enticing him, she handed him the letter with strict instructions that he was to give it to the bridegroom himself, and to no one else. This barber was extremely fond of talking and very charming in his own way, and he was also experienced in the ways of the world.

As soon as he left on this mission, my family and I began to hope; even the cruellest of husbands would help his wife. It was possible that my problems would be solved. An hour later he came back. He shook his head. He had not met with success. He did manage to get the letter to my husband, who did read it in private, but then somehow either he mentioned it to his family members, or they found out in some other way.

A lot of arguments ensued. The elders of the family stated very clearly that there was some cunning scheme afoot, that this might even involve injury or death of the groom. His family was able to influence him and he was told he could not visit me. The barber, Khalifa ji, also said that my husband was planning to show the letter to his friend, the police inspector.

When the barber tried to talk to him alone, his family chased him out. However, the old barber was not ready to give up yet. He said he was going to make another trip and would try to meet him alone. I was standing behind the doorway as the barber narrated the story to my mother.

Silent tears ran down my cheeks. I sighed and came back to my bedroom and lay down on my bed. My face buried in my pillow, I gave vent to my tears yet again.

I don't know how long I was lying there crying and thinking. It's possible I fell asleep. I was half asleep, half awake, all that had transpired running through my mind. I could see each scene in my mind's eye like a slideshow, starting from that fateful train ride. What was this all about if not just to destroy me—I had been violated and shamed with my family too sharing my shame.

I had no future, my family's good name was mired in the dirt and for me the worst was yet to come. I rolled over on my back, and with my teeth clenched, I started to curse my assailant. 'May the wrath of God descend upon him, may he suffer as I have, may his home and family be destroyed!' I could see his face in front of my eyes as I cursed him in anger.

I was writhing in my bed like a snake that had been pinned. I was still in that state when Amma Jaan came rushing into my room like a child and said in a strange voice, 'He is here.' And just as fast as she came, she disappeared.

For a moment I didn't understand what she was saying. Then it dawned on me that my husband had come to see me. I quickly covered myself with a light quilt, tidied the bed, then sat in one corner of the bed so that he could sit at the other end. I was waiting, my heart was beating violently,

I couldn't think straight and at the same time all kinds of thoughts were running through my head with great speed.

I kept thinking about how I was supposed to begin this conversation. I was still trying to figure that out when I heard a knock on the door. My head went down involuntarily, I covered my face with my chador. I heard the rustle of the curtain being pulled aside, then I heard the firm footsteps of a man entering my room.

I looked through the corner of my eye and I saw black shoes and silken trousers. I was still sitting in the same position in one corner. He sat down on the other side with his back towards me. I was quiet, I was thinking, dear God what am I supposed to say? How am I supposed to begin saying all this? He too was quiet. Who was going to start this conversation?

He cleared his throat. I lifted my head and thought I would take a quick look at my husband. There was a mirror on the other side of the room in which I could see his reflection. I saw that reflection.

I sprang up. I struck him hard on his back and shouted, 'You monster!'

Then, falling into the arms of my degenerate, deplorable, monstrous, abuser, my husband, I fainted. This was the man who had humiliated me, the same cruellest beloved whom I was cursing agonizingly a few minutes ago.

14

Suffering Becomes Its Own Solution

When I came to, I blinked, convinced that my eyes had deceived me.

'Is this all a dream? The same person who had assaulted me, is holding me in his arms? The same person who had made my life hell was here in my bedroom! Except that now he was looking at me with love in his eyes, with a smile on his lips, and was holding my face between his hands?'

I was still not fully recovered from my stupor. I wasn't sure if this was a dream, or a reality. I raised a trembling hand to touch his forehead.

My depraved, deceitful, cruel husband smiled at me and said, 'What are you looking at? You can see the scar where you hit me.'

My emotions were all muddled up, I was terrified. I was in disbelief, I was confused and elated! I was happy! I was saved!

I said, 'You have tortured me, I have suffered at your hands.' Tears gushed down my cheeks again. The thought that he might get up and leave me, frightened me. 'I'm not going to let you go,' I said as I firmly grasped his wrist. 'I am never going to let you go again,' I said in a tone filled with fear and resolve.

'Don't worry,' he replied. 'For God's sake, don't worry.' He hugged me.

'You have tortured me too much!' I exclaimed again.

He showed me his finger, smiled and said, 'See this is where you bit me. You don't know that I got an infection on my finger, it was extremely painful, I thought I was going to lose my finger. It didn't heal for three months.' He wagged his finger at me. 'You are a biter!' He was trying to make light of the situation.

I grabbed the lapels of his coat with both my hands. Then, wiping tears from my face, I shook him and pleaded, 'Take me with you now, please take me with you now! You have ruined my life! You are a complete degenerate! I have cursed you, and cursed you. You are a villain and a vagabond.'

'Stop this nonsense,' he said jokingly. 'After all, what have I done? Who has told you all this about me? They are completely wrong about me. Come, say something.'

I didn't say anything. I was really happy, blissfully happy. I was saved at last.

It suddenly dawned on me that I must tell my mother. I jumped up and ran to the door.

'Where to?' he asked.

I smiled at him, and said I was going to tell my mother.

'Wait,' he said. 'What are you going to say?'

'Why,' I said, 'I am going to tell her the truth, I'm going to tell her that the man who dishonoured and disrespected my father, my grandfather, is you. I want the black mark of disgrace that has become our identity, to deface you also.'

I ran to my mother. She was sitting on the prayer mat. I stood next to her. I saw her hands raised in prayer, she was crying bitterly, and cursing. 'Oh my Allah! This man who has destroyed us, may your wrath fall upon him.'

I quickly covered her mouth with my hands and said, 'No Amma, no! Please no more. Don't curse him, he is the one, he is the one.'

On hearing this my mother's eyes widened in surprise. After a moment she realized the full impact of what I had said to her. She became elated and in her excitement she let out a cry. Leaving her shoes behind she rushed to my father. I too ran behind her but I stopped at the door. She stood on her tiptoes and whispered the news to him. When he heard the news, my father passed out.

I returned to my room.

'So, you told your parents,' he said to me with a smile.

I looked at his face and the joy that I felt at being saved made me break into tears again. He put his arms around me. Holding me with great affection, he said, 'I'm going to leave now, but I will be back. You know I came here secretly, no one knows I'm here.'

'I'm not going to let you go,' I said. 'You will leave me again.'

I clung to him and wept. My wicked husband laughed and embraced me again, comforted me, he lovingly asked for my forgiveness and then he bid me goodbye. As he was leaving he said smilingly, 'Everything will soon be all right.'

He's gone now and I'm crying tears of joy.

Yours truly,

A fortunate girl.

Translator's Afterword

Vampire is set in 1930s India. The narrator, a young woman of sixteen, belongs to a conservative middle class Muslim family, has grown up within the confines of the four walls of her home, with little exposure to the outside world, and has few survival skills to exist as an independent person, except as someone's daughter, someone's sister, wife or mother. Because of a horrible accident of fate, she becomes an unwed pregnant woman, a victim of rape, a woman whose own family and community are not willing to accept her. This ostracization extends to her parents as well who are victims but are also participating members of a society that creates the tyranny of oppression.

Some readers of this narrative might feel that the last chapter has let them down. Why does the young woman experience relief and happiness after she discovers that her husband is the man who had raped her? We have read about her suffering, her sorrows, her shame, her feeling of guilt on having her father arrested and then his attempted suicide, making it clear to her that he preferred death to having a daughter in her present state. We have read about the indignities that she and her family have endured. She wants her suffering and her family's sufferings to stop, to end. She is scarred and broken for life, and she tells us that again and again, her story will never be a living happily-ever-after story.

But at that moment, when she is suddenly faced with the man who had raped her and who is now before her as a loving husband, all she can experience, after the initial feelings of shock, disbelief and anger, is intense relief. The letter to God ends there. We must contextualize the ending, view it in reference to the times in which the events take place, move away from what should be to what was, deviate from our own views about reactions to the narrator's plight to her reactions and the reasons for her behaviour. I can't help but think of Henrik Ibsen and his play *A Doll's House* and the story of alternate endings. He changed the ending to pacify a disgruntled audience: Nora does not leave her family, her husband and children, she stays. The modern reader would like the young woman in *Vampire* to shut the door on her husband and ... well, and what? A good story is one that leaves the reader pondering, wondering, and shaken. This is what *Vampire* does. We may have forgotten, as we continued to read, that the novel is really a long letter to God. The letter was written later, it is really a lament, a painful remembrance, and we cannot fail to see the irony in the way the narrator or the writer of the letter, ends the letter by referring to herself as 'The Fortunate One'.

Acknowledgements

This translation would not have been possible without Professor Tahira Naqvi's mentorship and her intellectual and emotional help. I and Mirza Azeem Baig Chughtai's grandchildren's are greatly indebted to her for helping introduce his work to an English readership. I am grateful for my husband Muhammad Saleem's support, reassurance and patience during the process of translation. Last but not least, I am fortunate to have Renuka Chatterjee as my editor, her calm, professional, steady hand is greatly appreciated.

WON'T YOU STAY, RADHIKA?

Usha Priyamvada

Translated by Daisy Rockwell

After her widowed father marries a younger woman, Radhika's world falls apart. She feels betrayed—the emotional and intellectual bond that she had forged with him since the early death of her mother breaks with that sudden marriage. To escape the unbearable situation at home—the growing rift between her and her father—Radhika moves to Chicago to pursue her master's in fine arts. She returns to India two years later, burdened by a sense of alienation and homesickness, only to realize that while nothing had changed in her country, everything had. The family that she had longed to be reunited with barely acknowledges her arrival. The sense of belonging is missing, leaving her in 'an emotional state of in-between-ness, of universal unbelonging'. As days pass, Radhika is paralysed with ennui, which tinges all her relationships—romantic or filial. So she lies on her takht, bored, immobile, uninspired...

An extraordinary chronicler of the inner lives of the urban Indian woman, Usha Priyamvada is a pioneering figure in modern Hindi literature. *Won't You Stay, Radhika?*, first published in 1967, expertly explores the stifling and narrow-minded social ideals that continue to trap so many Indian women in the complex web of individual freedom, and social and familial obligation. Daisy Rockwell's sensitive and skilful translation brings this poignant Hindi novel to a new set of readers.